DIES INFAUSTUS

Edited by

Shannon Iwanski

Dies Infaustus

*Nana + Grampie,
Thank you so much for
your love and support...
And for the kick in
the pants to keep
trying! This wouldn't
have been possible
without you!
Much love,
– Carmen
June 2018*

A Murder of Storytellers, llc.

Tulsa, Oklahoma

Edited by Shannon Iwanski

Cover Illustration by Alan Sessler

A Murder of Storytellers, llc.
P.O. Box 700391
Tulsa, Ok 74170
www.AMurderOfStorytellers.com

ISBN: 0-692-43332-5
ISBN-13: 978-0-692-43332-4

To those who fear what lies beneath the water's surface, and to those who cannot help but peek at the horrors of the deep.

CONTENTS

FROM THE LABOR OF GOD'S WORMS

by Christian Riley

Like a hinge, William's thoughts kept swinging back to the worms. His first encounter came in the form of a dream, exactly one year to the day after Jenny's disappearance. In this vision William observed Earth from space. The planet was a bluish-green orb with a surface that bulged and retracted, indicative of the great squirming within—the movements of such god-like creatures as they tunneled through the planets' core. Ultimately, this dream would prove recurrent, plaguing William with profound frequency—nightly, daily, anytime he so much as closed his eyes for rest. But it was only a dream. And of the worms, they found other means to enter into William's mind.

Of course, he saw them in the foods he ate. Noodles and rice were no longer on the menu, but this mattered little. A side of beef, a baked potato, some blanched asparagus—all vague pretexts of nourishment, as William saw them for what they might have really been: seared circular muscle layer; bloated and cracked septum; green nematodes pulled from the sea… They were all worms.

His front lawn crawled with them. Each blade of grass, linear in structure, was a worm. Even the clouds above adopted this form, a massive cumulus describing the soft, opaque clitellum of a night-crawler. As parts of a whole, the universe itself suggested the overwhelming presence of something worm-like in nature: spiral galaxies, the circular orbits of countless suns and satellites, black-holes and *wormholes*—were they not each of them a ghostly hint of something that bores and curls, that draws its winding, sightless path into the depths of eternity?

William certainly thought so. He found himself mulling over

1

these thoughts day and night, as they served as impressions of something tangible in a world that made little sense to him anymore. Since the day he and his wife realized their greatest form of grief, (then later, and with more clarity, after the worms had tunneled holes into his head), all that mattered to William was the memory of his daughter, and of the prospect that one day, he and his wife would find some type of closure. That one day, despite the inherent horror and dread, William and Madeline would find a fragment of their daughter's corpse, and that they would at last grant this find to its rightful place: into the family plot, into the soil below, with its many and more waiting, wriggling, ravenous worms.

Jennifer Anne Haley—the daughter—disappeared on a Saturday morning, while looking for seashells along a rocky beach in northern Washington. William and Madeline were only one hundred feet away when the sneaker wave took the girl. William ran into the water after hearing the crash and flailed against the current for what seemed like hours, almost drowning himself, before struggling back to land. Later, the authorities helped with the search, but they never found Jennifer—not ever—and the ensuing desperation for that final closure pulled at the seams that, for almost two decades, had bound William and Madeline's marriage. Jennifer was but a child, their only child, and her absence devastated the couple. William in particular let himself go, let certain pieces of his life fall to the ground like dust. After a year, his dreams and visions—the worms—they appeared and had become an obsession for him. Then, after two years, it was all William could do just to get himself up in the morning, get to work, sustain his body with coffee, perhaps a little rum in the evening. Anything beyond this was a mountain, and somewhere high up a cliff dangled his wife. The culmination of their loss and pain, along with the brutal passage of time, as it leeched away any and all possibilities of finding Jenny—the culmination had created a stark void in their marriage, a yawning gap which only became accentuated with William's growing mania.

And now, miracle of miracles…

Halfway around the world, just outside Norilsk, Russia, a group of meteorite hunters stumbled across the SS *Hydrus*. From a distance the four-hundred-foot, steel-hulled freighter looked like a small hill, albeit lacking the expected cover of snow. Upon closer examination the hunters found the entire ship encased in a massive block of ice, with a corrugated base spanning the perimeter—as if the earth itself had given birth to the aberration. And an aberration it was, as it had been over one hundred years since anyone had last seen the SS *Hydrus*…the day she sank to the bottom of Lake Huron.

"It's like, a piece of a puzzle," William said, reading the news on his laptop. "The lost piece, you know? The one that got sucked up the vacuum cleaner, or something."

"I guess," replied Madeline. Her voice sounded reticent, lethargic, tired now of speaking from across the void.

William turned away from her, from his laptop, and searched for his beer. There was something on his mind, something beyond the worms that he couldn't quite pinpoint, and damn if his wife was going to help him any. He found the bottle of Heineken on the kitchen counter, where he had left it, after his eye had caught the article on his computer. The beer was now lukewarm, but he took a drink anyway, and then looked at his wife. He stared at her until she grew uncomfortable; he saw that on her face. "I don't know, Maddie," William said, peeling his eyes away from her. "To tell the truth, it's kind of scary."

After a pause, Madeline said, "I've got some errands to run." She went to the door with her purse and keys, gave a sigh, and then said, "I'll see you tonight."

❧❦❧❦❧❦

A week later...

"They found another one, Maddie." William's eyes were glued once again to the screen of his laptop. His throat felt tight as a drum, his hands were moist and sticky, as if they had been immersed in seawater. "They found an airplane somewhere in Mexico."

"So I heard," replied Madeline. She was in the kitchen with a glass of wine in one hand, absently wiping at a stain in the counter grout with the other.

William supposed it was all still too new for her, too bizarre. He considered his wife's skepticism, though he hated it. "This plane," he continued, "it disappeared in 1948. Had thirty-six passengers on it, and they say it went down in the Bermuda Triangle." William stood and took a step toward his wife, unable to hold back his enthusiasm, despite her unspoken objection—an objection to the path they both knew he'd been traveling on. It was the same path since the tragedy, only now, things had grown much faster, faster than the crawling of the worms. "The Bermuda Triangle, Madeline...that's in the ocean. Like the other one—that ship in Russia—the plane disappeared in the ocean."

Specifically, the plane was a Douglas DC-3 with a last known whereabouts somewhere off the coast of Miami, some sixty-five years ago—until an old man discovered it behind his house, in Jicayan, Mexico: a colossal ice cube that had sprouted sometime in the night. Everything about the plane's condition was identical to that of the SS *Hydrus*, with one exception: the passengers were still inside. When the proper officials finally arrived upon the village, a horde of Jicayan men were three-quarters into the plane with pickaxes. Several bodies were thawing on a tarp outside, slabs of meat, their shapes still contorted to match the void between their seats. Huddled nearby was a group of old women, praying none-too-softly.

William stared at his wife, stared at her long and hard, looking for something on that blank slate she was so fond of portraying. "They found the bodies, Maddie. The bodies from the ocean. Don't you get it?"

※ ※ ※

There had been a brief attempt from certain governments to snuff out the media coverage of the strange discoveries—concerns of mass hysteria. But it wasn't long before these efforts proved ineffectual. After two more planes had been found in remote areas, (one in the mountains of Chile, another in Nepal), Alaska's "Phantom Ship," the SS *Baychimo*, unearthed itself five miles north of Las Vegas, Nevada. Last seen when abandoned to pack ice in 1969, the large vessel was almost completely thawed upon her discovery. There were no bodies inside, of course, but this detail had little effect on William's mounting optimism.

"What if, Maddie?" William said. He ran his fingers through his hair, picked up a thick layer of grease.

"What if, *what*?" she replied—she *finally* replied.

"You know—what if they find her? In a block of ice somewhere, and—"

"And nothing! She's dead, William. She's never coming back." Madeline covered her face with both hands and wiped outward, smearing tears across her cheeks. She looked at her husband, stabbed him with her stare, cold steel in her eyes. "You ask me, '*What if?*' You haven't slept with me in six months... What if you did that?"

⁂

At last, a variant of the global phenomenon occurred one morning, outside a cafe in Salerno, Italy. It was the discovery of a single human body encased in ice, naked, arms clamped to the sides, eyes wide, wholesome and seemingly alive. After painstaking efforts the man was eventually identified as one Jason Colburn, who had gone missing ten years prior, while on a sailing trip across the English Channel.

William was beside himself with emotion after he read the news. He stood in the corner of the living room that night, in the dark, crying for all the wonders of the universe. *Such possibilities, wide as God's own hand...* When this revelation came, it made William cry even louder, made him wail. His mind worked laboriously to put together all the pieces. He thought of his dream then, of certain entities—God's creations—crawling wormlike inside the earth, toting all those things long since forgotten, pulling them from great black caverns: the storage rooms that housed a million lost souls trapped in ice.

"Maddie, I've got it!" he called. His voice was raspy, his eyes blurred, wet with tears. "Maddie, where are you?" Silence came from down the hall, and he remembered that his wife had gone to the movies with her friends. "Why aren't you here, Maddie? You should be here right now."

⁂

Three weeks later a website went up, sponsored by an international agency, on behalf of things long since forgotten, and

5

for the benefit of those who would remember. William bookmarked the page, began checking it daily, hourly, by the minute. Since the arrival of Jason Colburn, thirty-five human popsicles subsequently rose in the night, across the globe, along with ten more ships, and fourteen planes, all of which had at one time succumbed to the watery depths of the world. And that was only what had been discovered. William envisioned, with exquisite horror, his daughter's well-persevered corpse swiftly melting somewhere in the vast Sahara Desert, no eyes to bear witness to her arrival save for that of the blazing sun, and a few hungry vultures.

Ironically, before he found the website, William had stepped away from his obsession for a few days, even shaved, stopped calling in sick to work. His wife cooked dinner on one of these nights, and he enjoyed her quaint smile in the kitchen. There was a reconciled affect about her movements, the way she worked the knife, how she chopped and diced and casually transferred consumables from one place to the next. They even laughed together. It was almost as if they were young again, or so William recalled, and as he looked at his wife he remembered lost details of their marriage, precious moments of a time long before the tragedy...

But then the website went up, and it was back to God's worms and black caverns and frozen packages slithering in his mind.

"It can really happen, Maddie! It can *really* happen!"

❧❧❧

As subtle as it began, it ended. With every scientist on earth in a mad fervor over solving the riddle, and the whole world biting nails day in and day out, and William withering away in the corner with his laptop, the "reappearances" just stopped. Days went by, then weeks, and still—nothing. The suspense was maddening for William, (let alone all of humanity), and his thoughts of a finale to this magnificent mechanism of space and time drove a six inch knife into his gut.

"We've lost her again, Maddie!" he screamed, somewhere in the dark confines of his house, his lonely house. His wife was no longer there to hear him. He wasn't sure where she was, where she'd gone, running in denial as always, he presumed. At last, the void between them had become cosmic in size, fathomless, immeasurable. Perhaps Madeline had left him, left him for good, this time. But William hardly cared anymore. Because in the dark, behind his eyes, he saw little pictures of his daughter. He saw her riding in a black ocean with fantastic worms rolling in and out, between her limbs, carrying her through the shadows of the deep. He saw her eyes blink, and he knew that Jennifer was still alive, somewhere down there...*somewhere right here, here on earth.*

William screamed and pulled at his hair, thought he might yank the pictures out of his mind, lay them on the ground before his feet, make them come alive. In this tantrum, he smashed his fist through his laptop and hurled shards of plastic across the room. He cursed his own breath and felt cold, so cold. He found a jacket and slipped it on, left the house in a storm of obscenities, and stepped into the pouring rain, with its dollops of thick round water, heavy as the black ocean beyond—the same ocean that stole Jennifer and that hides those great worms...*God's worms.*

"We lost Jenny!" he kept screaming, over, and over, and over again.

☠☠☠

The night was strong in its blackness, but William saw the ocean all the same, saw it as much as he heard it. And the sound might as well have been Jenny's own voice whispering into his ears.

Or Madeline's.

Or perhaps even God's.

William took a step forward and then stopped, kicked off his shoes, pulled off his socks. The mouth of the Pacific nipped at his feet, sharp rocks like teeth bit into his soles as he continued to walk forward. "I'll find her, Maddie," he whispered, as he met the waves. The touch of the cold water was a dull knife across his ankles. "I'll find our little girl...I'll do it, I swear."

Waist deep now, William felt the entire mass of earth's ocean coddle him. It pushed and pulled, guided him forward, poured the secrets of the deep into his ears. And with crashing roars, it promised him victory. There was a visceral tug upon his legs, and this he thought were the worms, the worms at last. They had come for him—they found him. They lurched forward, and in the end he went with them, into their final embrace, with their cold caress, and the pull of the great black sea, down, down into the cavernous depths. Down to find his daughter.

  As abruptly as it had ended, it began once again. In the plaza of Santa Fe, New Mexico, on the street in front of the Palace of the Governors, they found another body: a young girl. She stood erect, and like all the others, was encased in ice. Her arms were crossed against her chest, her hands lay flat against her shoulders, and her stare was haunting and wide, locked magnificently onto the vast blue sky.

SEA IS IN MY BLOOD

by Deborah Walker

Julia studied the body of the dead fish lying on the marble slab of the work surface. How should she transform this piece of cold flesh? Even before her ministrations, the underside of the ray bore a striking resemblance to a grotesque human face. The fish's nostrils might be large, blank, empty eyes, and the wide-toothed mouth grinned in a silent leer. The image came to her. This fish would become a bishop. She took out her steel boning knife and began to carve. There was artistry involved here. As she made her swift cuts, Julia saw the future. She visualised the effect that would occur once the fish dried, the changing and warping that would occur as the moisture dried into the air. Julia fashioned the fish with those changes in mind. She understood the final decorations that time would add to her work.

She cut the pectoral fins away from the head and moulded them into a headdress that would resemble a mitre. She cut at the ventral fins and pulled them into a shape that might resemble legs. She cut away the ray's tail; a bishop had no need of a tail. And, finally, she inserted black beads into the nostrils to resemble pupils and pulled at the flesh of the fish, carefully shaping the emerging expression.

The newly created bishop stared at her with its bead eyes, but she had no time to study it. She slid it on to the drying tray. Julia had many more monsters to create.

The old fashioned bell of the door rang. Julia wiped her hands on her canvas apron and walked through the workshop to the front of the shop.

Two women, dressed in their protective tourists suits, entered.

"How wonderful," said the tall woman, twirling around to look at monsters arranged on the wall.

"How wonderfully old-fashioned," agreed the small woman,

breathing in the scent of varnish in the air.

Julia smiled at the women. "Please take your time to browse. I can answer any questions you might have."

"They're Jenny Hanivers, aren't they?"

"Yes, Ma'am."

"How wonderful." The small woman fingered the hard, dried flesh of the Jenny Hanivers displayed on the counter. "Did you make them yourself?"

"I made some of them. My mother also crafts them, and my father... some of the works are my father's."

"Your father, yes, I see." The tall tourist looked at Julia with a look of understanding.

Carved and dried, the Jenny Hanivers looked down upon the tourists—mermaids, dragons, basilisks, bishops—the once living creature, harvested from the sea, then mutilated into a new shape to spend an afterlife as a glazed dream. These were souvenirs for tourists with a taste for the macabre.

"Will the men be at the dock?" asked the tall women.

This was the reason tourists came to Shipsdown. They came in bus loads to see the infected men of the docks, to buy their strange shells and to listen to their stories. If it wasn't for the men of the docks, there would be no tourist industry

"The men are always at the docks," said Julia, smiling. "They'll be glad of your support."

"I can't wait to see them," said the tall woman. "What's this one?" She pointed to a Jenny Haniver that had caught her eye.

"It's a mermaid," said Julia. "In the old days, the Hanivers were seen as proof of the existence of all sorts of strange creatures. Sailors would buy them and take them home, spreading the tales of the sea to the land."

"It's very finely made. Perhaps we'll call back, after we've seen the men."

"You'll be welcome," said Julia. "Goodbye."

"Goodbye, my dear."

Julia sighed. She had felt sure that woman was going to buy a Haniver. The tall woman had looked at the mermaid with an intensity that often preceded a sale. She would have bought it if she'd been here on her own. Perhaps she would come back, without her friend. But the tourists seldom came back.

Julia went back to the workshop. The dead fish were slowly transformed into what the tourists called folk art. After a time, rows and rows of Jenny Hanivers were laid out on the drying boards.

"Mum, I'm finished. I'm going out." Julia shouted upstairs. No doubt her mother was staring into her silver edged mirror, a wedding gift from Father.

"Hold on," shouted her mother. Mother came down the stairs slowly and entered the workshop. She was a hard-faced woman, her mouth pressed into a lipstick grimace, a slash of vermillion in stone tinged skin. Mother's face had been drying and changing, these past two years. Somehow, it always managed to surprise Julia, these changes in her mother. She had seen her mother staring at her image for hours, trying to see something different in the mirror. What was she looking for? Was it something she could ever find?

Let me see anything, but not this face destroyed by the harsh salt air—desiccated and unloved.

"Did I hear the shop bell ring?" asked Mother, breaking into Julia's speculations.

"Two tourists came in, but they didn't buy anything."

"Hmmmm."

"They said that they'd be back."

"Hmmmm."

Her mother inspected Julia's work. She had only just allowed Julia to work on the fish these past six months. There had been a small ceremony, of sorts, when Julia had turned sixteen. "Now you're old enough," her mother had said, as Julia had unwrapped the boning knife that had served as her birthday present. "You're old enough to understand what needs to be done, to create the Hanivers."

"It's good work," said her mother, casting her practiced eyes over the rows of dead fish. "How many have you done?"

"Ten mermaids, five angels, thirty devils, and five bishops."

"That's about the right ratio," said her mother. "No dragons?"

"We've still got two dozen dragons in the shop."

"Good work. I'll set them to dry and you can have the rest of the day off. This rain will keep off most of the tourists. I can manage on my own this afternoon."

"Thanks, Mum," said Julia, wiping her hands clean.

"Don't go down to the docks though."

"Mum, of course not," said Julia, striving for authenticity in her lies. She ran upstairs to change out of her work clothes.

When she came down she saw that her mother was examining her face in a small make-up mirror.

"Don't do that, Mum," said Julia.

"Do what?" Mother put the mirror into her handbag. "I'm sorry we have to stay here, Julia."

"Mum, it's all right—really."

"We make a good living here, don't we? I just don't know if we'll be able to live anywhere else. I'm not ready to move on, yet."

It had been two years since Julia's father had been lost to them.

"Mum, I like it here. Don't worry. I understand, you know."

"But, I do worry. Sometimes I think that we should get away. I worry, Julia, all the time."

Julia saw that her mother was reaching into her handbag again, seeking out her mirror. Julia needed to get out of the shop, out of the smell of dead fish and varnish, the smell of transformation. She just didn't want to have this conversation again.

"Mum, it's okay. I'll see you later. I won't be long." Julia opened the shop door quickly, almost knocking the spring bound bell off its wire.

"Don't go to the docks," said her mother as she began to set out the dead fish to dry in front of the clay oven.

❧❧❧

Julia walked along the edge of the old stone dock. She wasn't supposed to be here and that's what made it so exciting.

Her mother had been right; the rain had kept most of the tourists away. But there were a few, walking along the dock, taking in the sights.

"Hello, Julia." It was one of the men.

"Hello, Mr. Crackle. How's business?"

"Passing slow."

Julia stepped aside as a couple of tourists paused in front of Mr. Crackle.

Julia looked at their foolish tourist suits. Nobody knew how the disease was passed. Some people believed you had to touch one of the infected fish, but that was unlikely. Fishing had been banned for eighteen months now. The boats stood rotting in the harbour;

each day brought another layer of decay, and the lichens rose up covering them with a cloth of green and blue and mustard yellow, and still new cases of infection were found.

But the tourists were careful, wearing their plastic suits against the threat of sickness. Still, it was one more source of income for this dying town. Now that the fish industry had died, tourism was the only way to make a living.

Julia was wearing a dress with a bright red flower print. She wasn't a tourist. She lived here.

"Will I sing for you?" Mr. Crackle asked the tourists. They nodded. Within their plastic suits Julia made out the form of a man. Julia was surprised. The tourists were usually women; women couldn't catch the disease—or so the Government said.

> Sails of silk, and ropes of sandal,
> Such as gleam in ancient lore;
> And the singing of the sailors,
> And the answer from the shore.

The threaded reed of Mr. Crackle's voice came to a halt. The tourists waited for a moment, as if unsure if that was all they would get, but it was.

"Thank you," said the tourist man. He put a five-pound note into Mr. Crackle's tin cup, and they moved away.

"That was beautiful, Mr. Crackle. Did you make it up?"

"No, love. A fellow called Longfellow wrote it a long time ago. I added it to one of the old shanties, it seemed to fit."

"You were never at sea, were you, Mr. Crackle?"

"No, Julia."

He reached out his strange hands to remove the note from the tin. His hands were corrupted by the infection which merged with the code of a man's body to produce something new. Or perhaps, the disease resurrected the old data, the messages of the sea that swims in us all and had been only been forgotten—but was now remembered in the shape of a fully scaled hand.

"I used to own the coffee house. But nobody wants to buy drinks from the infected. Still, the sea is in my blood now. I remember things, the songs, they come from somewhere."

"I know what you mean," said Julia. She hummed a fragment

of the melody. "They are very beautiful, aren't they—the old songs?"

"You understand, don't you Julia, and yet you're a woman. How very strange."

"Am I strange, Mr. Crackle? The world is strange to me," said Julia, still humming a fragment of his melody. "The seas are poisoned, the fish are dying, and changes are all around. The Government can't control anything, let alone the disease that has grown and multiplied on our coast. Maybe I'm strange, or maybe I'm not."

Mr. Crackle looked closely at Julia, and she saw that the disease had progressed to his face, hardening the flesh and recreating it in the image of something other.

Last month, Julia had seen a man looking out on the dock with the eyes of a fish. She had wanted to talk to him. She had wondered what he saw through those strange eyes. But the Government had taken him away before she had a chance to ask.

"Well, take care, Mr. Crackle. I enjoyed your song."

"And you got it for free," he laughed. "Come back again soon, Julia."

"I will."

⚜⚜⚜

Julia knew all of the men on the dock. She used to come here with her father. The men, in their various states of transformation, sat on the edge of the dock; their souvenirs were laid out in front of them, shells and driftwood, the flotsam of the sea.

Julia watched the gazing gaping tourists. Every now and again, a tourist would let out a cry when they saw a particularly strange twist of flesh. The men of the dock were usually old, with their faces ravaged by years of sea spray, washing away, to produce the hard crags of their faces, as if the flesh of their faces had turned to rock. Then, on top of this change came the new corruption, the disease.

"Here's a pretty shell for a pretty lady." A new voice called along the dock, a young voice. The voice surprised her. Julia caught sight of the shell waved in her direction; it was an iridescent gift.

"Hello," said Julia, staring like a tourist. This man *was* young. His face had not yet succumbed to the inevitable petrifaction of the sea, and the scales of his face gleamed in the air. He was quite beautiful. This is what the disease looked like, then, when it caught the scent of youth.

She did know him. It was Michael Kenwood. He was a couple of years older than her. She'd seen him at school—before they'd closed it down a year ago.

"Michael, hi."

Julia was surprised; she thought that all the young men had left Shipsdown.

Don't go near the fish men. Her mother had warned her time and time again. "They harbour all types of dangers for someone like you." Julia had never understood the warnings—until now.

"Hello," he said. Michael was sitting on a square of tarpaulin. He moved his body to reach up to her, and in that movement, she saw the flashing of a shoal of fish.

Julia wondered what had kept him in Shipsdown. A girlfriend, perhaps? She looked at his face. No—it must be his old mother, keeping him here. He had stayed behind to care for her.

"Will you buy a shell?"

"What?" Michael's voice had broken the day-dreams that were sweeping over her. "How much?" she remembered to say.

"One pound for you, but I wish I could give it away."

"It's all right. I know you people don't have much money." A wave of embarrassment coursed over her. Why did she say that? It was her mother. Her mother's prejudices were lettered irrevocably through Julia, no matter how much she tried to escape them. Her mother's constant teachings had cast a net over her daughter's thoughts.

But Michael appeared not to notice and only held out the shell, patient as the sea.

"You've carved it, how lovely. Please, wait a minute."

Julia stopped to pull on her gloves. She wished she didn't have to. It seemed so rude. But she'd promised her mother that she'd never touch a man without protection. She wished she'd thought to put them on before she came out.

"It's all right," said Michael seeing her hesitate. "It's only sensible. Who knows? You might be infected, you might be protecting me."

They laughed together at this small joke, as if she could be infected; she was so clean and silky, smooth; she was a woman.

Julia took the shell and passed him over the pound coin. She turned the shell carefully, examining the carvings. "Oh, it's a Jenny Haniver. We sell these to the tourists."

"It's a sea dreamer."

"I've never heard them called that before."

The small carving was delicate, delineating an image that was both grotesque and beautiful, rendered deeply into the surface of the shell.

"She sings in my dreams. I saw her, once, when I was out fishing. She rose out of the sea and called to me. Listen to her song,

> *Sails of silk, and ropes of sandal,*
> *Such as gleam in ancient lore;*
> *And the singing of the sailors,*
> *And the answer from the shore.*

It was the song that Mr. Crackle had sung an hour ago.

"It's a beautiful song. Did Mr. Crackle teach it to you?"

"It's the song she always sings, although she doesn't sing in words, of course. This is just our poor interpretation."

His belief was so insistent, his confidence so strong, that she found herself slipping into his shell of certainty.

"Did you want to join her?" asked Julia.

"I did, but I had strong ties to the land, then. But now, now, I think there's not much to hold me here."

"I'm sorry," said Julia. She found herself staring at his face, at the silvered scales that circled his eyes. She wondered how much of his body was covered in the gleaming flesh. "Where have you been? I've not seen you for a long time—since they closed the school."

"I've been staying in Starmouth—not too far away. I've had the sea dreamer's touch for nigh on six months, but she calls us all here. This will be her place of resurrection, I reckon."

For a moment longer he held Julia in the spell of his story, but then she smiled. She knew that the men liked to weave tales, explaining their disease.

"I'm not a tourist, you know."

"Listen to the shell."

"Will I hear the sea dreamer?"

16

"I think you will. A shell carved with the sea dreamer will speak to you. She comes from before, before we poisoned the sea. I have the memory of her. Listen to the sea dreamer, Julia."

Michael was becoming agitated. The pleasant encounter, the shared magic of the tale was turning to something else.

"Julia!" It was her mother's voice coming along the dock. "What are you doing here?" Her mother grabbed her arm. "I've told you not to talk to these people, it's not safe."

Quickly Julia pushed the shell into her pocket.

"I'm sorry," she apologised. She reached into her purse and took out a five pound note and held it out for him.

"I don't take charity," he said.

"It's for your mother."

He looked bemused.

"Quickly, take it."

But he didn't, and her mother pulled her away.

Her mother was so angry. She walked away from the dock, pulling Julia behind her. Julia began to cry.

But something was strange—all over the dock she could hear that same song rising, and the tourist women were pushing off their protective hoods and holding something to their ears. Julia wanted to stay, but her mother's hold on her was relentless.

❦❦❦

"It's bad enough that we have to stay here. I need you to help me, Julia. This is a bad time for me," said her mother. "You've let me down badly."

"I'm sorry, Mum. I need to be on my own sometimes."

"Not down there. You weren't alone, down there. You were making a fine show for them all. They were all looking at you, especially that young one. Did you touch him?"

"No."

"Did he touch you? Tell me the truth."

"No."

"They're freaks. Stay away from them; they'll corrupt you."

"They're not freaks," shouted Julia. "They're like Dad. Was Dad a freak?"

"Yes, yes, he was. He used to touch me with his scaled hand,

and I couldn't bear it. I was glad when they took him away."

Her mother gave Julia a look full of hatred. It was a curious expression to see on the face of your mother.

☠☠☠

Her mother had left Julia. Her mother was upstairs lying down.

Julia took out the shell Michael had given her. It wasn't quite empty. There was a touch of silver substance in the peak of the spiral. She held it up to her ear, and she shuddered as she felt a needle-thin tongue of pain.

Everything changed.

Julia felt the tiny Hanivers invading her flesh. The sea dreamer had found a way to answer the call of the men. The Hanivers swam in Julia's blood, and they sang out.

Julia sat in the shop—listening to the Hanivers calling her out of this life and into somewhere strange and ancient.

An aspect of the old Julia said, "You're not real."

The Hanivers answered, "We are real now. We are ocean and land."

"I don't want it." Fainter now, the old Julia, the real Julia was slipping, slipping away.

"But you do want it, Julia. That is why you listened to the shell."

This is what it felt like to be infected, with the strange new disease that had crossed over from the sea creatures to man and, finally, to woman. The salt in her blood sang.

Like the constant moving sea, the sea dreamer had changed. She couldn't touch the bodies of the women, so she touched their minds instead. The molecules of the dreamer were coursing through the sea of Julia's blood, and swimming in her mind.

Outside the shop, Julia could see the men walking. They had left the docks, and their voices rose in the old song.

Sails of silk, and ropes of sandal,
Such as gleam in ancient lore;
And the singing of the sailors,
And the answer from the shore.

Soon the men would come for Julia. They would touch her skin with their scaled hands, but, first, she must make herself beautiful for them.

Julia took out her boning knife and began to cut her face, making it as beautiful as a mermaid. The tiny Jenny Hanivers ran down in her salt, blood-red tears.

Julia would be the most beautiful of all, because she knew how the cuts would look when they dried and changed. Julia cut her face, not only with the knowledge of what is, but what will be.

Soon, she would be dried and complete.

SINGING AT THE GREAT WALL OF THE OCEAN

by Chris Kuriata

Old Mrs. Duguay loaded our rowboat with quilts and a jug of white lightning before kicking off from the village pier a little after midnight, approximately fifteen minutes into my sixteenth birthday. We grabbed the oars and stroke-stroke-stroked past the first marker. Seaweed clung to our bow. Once the current seized hold of our creaky vessel, Mrs. Duguay dropped her oars and relaxed. Had she been wearing a hat she would have pulled the brim over her eyes, content to sleep all the way to the Great Wall of the Ocean.

I had questions. "Why isn't Mom coming?"

Mrs. Duguay plucked the cork from her jug. Alcoholic fumes made the moonlight waver. "It's late. She needs her rest."

Rest? Not to brag, but our midnight excursion was kind of a big deal. Ceremonial trips to the Great Wall of the Ocean happened only once a decade. People were jealous when our family won the lottery choosing me to represent the village. For weeks, a simple walk through the town square focused all eyes on me. At the very least, you'd think Mom would have wanted to see me in the fancy white gown Mrs. Duguay brought for me to wear.

Waves lifted the boat. The bow smacked the water and cold spray salted my lips. Feeling enchanted beneath the night sky, I began to sing:

> *The Jungfrau's crew, buried 'neath the waves*
> *Their tombstones marking empty graves*
> *On rocky floors, starved flesh is shorn*
> *Hollow bones float home, washed on the shore*

Everyone in the village despised my singing. "It's awful grim," they said. I shrugged off their criticism, taking confidence from the fact I only sang the truth. Every family had given up husbands, brothers, and sons to the hungry ocean. The sea has few stories of triumph, only endurance in the face of crooked odds. I suppose no one wanted to be reminded of that sad fact.

We learned about the Great Wall in school, but the drawings in our text books left me unprepared for the majesty of seeing her stone barrier in person, rising from the black water like the fin of a leviathan hungry enough to swallow the world.

I wish I'd exclaimed something more respectful than, "By my troth and maidenhead!"

Heavy blocks, enough to build a thousand pyramids, stretched in either direction until disappearing into the horizon. Local history contained a dozen sad stories about boats sailing along the edge of the wall, looking for gaps, but any discoveries remained secret. Only broken sails and hollow bones floated home from these failed explorations.

According to the fishermen along the pier, fresh fish crowded the waters on the other side of the Wall. Fish bigger and meatier than anything our village nets caught. Over the wall promised a bounty that would put an end to our food depression in a big hurry.

The current pulled our boat, and I feared we'd collide with the Wall and splinter into a hundred pieces, but Mrs. Duguay tickled the water with her oars and guided us to a peaceful bump against the algae splattered stone.

"Climb," Mrs. Duguay instructed.

I don't know what I was expecting. A ladder? Steps carved into the stone? I stood up, teetering wildly in my high heels, still uncertain of my role in this celebration. My fingers fit into the cracks between the stone. Praying not to slip, I hoisted myself out of the boat and began climbing the Wall.

Mrs. Duguay hollered beneath me, her voice softening as I made my way higher. "Look at you, Ann Darrow! You can do it!" I dared not look down, afraid of tempting the Gods of misfortune, who'd happily steal my balance and flick me off the Wall.

One shoe dropped. It hit the water after a delay, the splash sounding like a pebble landing in a puddle. I kicked the other shoes off. Barefoot, I made the last leg of the climb more easily. My big toe plugged into the cracks and supported me while I threw my arm over the top of the Wall and hauled myself onto the dry, cool stone.

I waved my hands, calling—no, bragging—"Look Mrs. Duguay! I made it!" No response came from below.

"Mrs. Duguay?"

All I could see was black water crashing against the Wall, and I feared a wave had claimed the boat, pulling Mrs. Duguay's heavy belly to the bottom of the ocean.

"Mrs. Duguay!"

Tears were about to come, but I spotted a glint of moonlight reflecting off Mrs. Duguay's jug. She lay safely in the boat, swaddled in the quilts, rowing all four oars against the tide, pushing her way back home, leaving me stranded barefoot and shivering atop the Great Wall of the Ocean.

Standing alone atop the Wall, I recalled Uncle Lou's instructions to surviving a capsized boat. The first rung on the ladder of survival was *not panicking*!

"Panicked lungs open right up," Uncle Lou said. "They fill with water and drag you down."

To keep my mind treading water, I took inventory of my narrow surroundings. The Wall's edges were crowded with bird nests. I suppose the Wall was a safe place to hatch their young safe from hungry predators. I peered into a few nests but saw no eggs. If Mrs. Duguay didn't return, I'd have to find another source for my breakfast.

Worries about my appetite soon disappeared. Beneath the water, something collided with the Wall. The reverberations dropped me to my knees on the rough stone. My skin bruised and the dress ripped. The Wall continued to shake until it felt like I was crouched on something alive.

Singing seemed the best way to stifle my panic.

The Captain dreams of full nets
While his crew is weary and ailed
And wives dream of ships returning
Carrying more men than originally sailed

Whatever lurked beneath the waves (a whale? an iron knocker?) banged into the Wall a second time and the ocean began to swell. Under the light of the moon, the water rose like oven dough, subsuming the Wall, reaching closer and closer for me.

My God, was this a tsunami? I thought of our sleeping village and despaired. The entire coast must be under water. Everything washed away.

An angry noise rattled the stone beneath my bare feet, a *clank-clank-clank* of sturdy cogs. The water wasn't rising, the Wall was lowering, delivering me into the ocean. Soon, I stood knee deep, holding the hem of my dress above my waist, feeling the cool rush of water as the bird nests floated away.

This made me—as far as I knew—the first woman to dip her toe into the ocean beyond the Wall. I'd be famous. A pioneer in the field of exploration, like Samuel Champlain. I bet they'd commemorate me in song.

My fantasy became interrupted when a grotesque black tube, rough with barnacles, shot out of the water and traced the edge of the Wall. A long series of bubbles burped to the surface from some Satanic blowhole, turning the air as pungent as rotting sea fare.

Oh, my stupid sixteen-year-old thoughts! Full of hope and vanity. How embarrassing I believed, even for a moment, that I was the first to place her foot on the other side of the Wall. Had I forgotten the other girls selected to perform this ritual long before me? Perhaps I willed myself to forget about them, those sixteen-year-old girls whose hallow bones floated home every ten years.

The stone cogs made a final rotation and the Wall lowered until the water reached my chin, leaving my pretty round head bobbing in the middle of the ocean. I thought this must be how the moon feels, all alone in the dark, too far for anyone to hear her song.

A desperate rescue plan popped into mind. If I shed this constrictive dress, I could swim back to shore. How far could it be? Birds traveled to make their nests here, and I refused to believe myself weaker than a bird.

Before I could make a break for it, something cold and powerful wrapped around my leg. The tentacle squeezed, cutting off the blood flow and putting my foot to sleep. Beneath the water, my numb toes turned purple, soon black.

The ocean no longer felt as lonely as it had a moment before. I sensed enormous life in the water. Beyond the tentacle lay the true shape of the sea beast, perhaps as tall as the Wall itself. I imagined a gaping maw, studded with sabre teeth, the gums leaking a slimy ooze to lubricate prey for easy passage into its belly. It must be hungry. Likely ten years had passed since the last young girl found herself lowered into the water.

Behind me, a distant clanging erupted from the direction of shore. I struggled to turn my head for a glimpse of the approaching boats. Points of light—as many as two dozen—were accompanied by the flapping sails and the creak of dry nets.

Every fishing vessel in the village rushed towards the Wall. My hope hadn't been misplaced after all. They were coming to rescue me. Someone must have gotten wind of Mrs. Duguay's devotion to this archaic ritual, and decided enough was enough.

I pulled against the tentacle, struggling to free myself but the beast held tight. More air bubbled to the surface and the water broke, birthing an enormous eye. It sat on the horizon, looking as red and wide as the sun setting into the sea. The plate-sized pupil dilated, focusing on me.

The approaching boats were still a ways off. How would their spotlights ever find me—a dark head bobbing in the middle of an infinite sea? It was up to me to guide them.

So I began to sing. I sang the song of our village, our history, and our endurance in the face of a sea that never produced enough fish to feed us. A sea without stories of triumph, only misery and loss.

The son of a hungry man
Sired to replace his hand
Will never haul heavier nets than his father
Even when he grows up to be stronger

Cold, briny air filled my lungs. I sang big enough to echo off the moon. They might even have heard me on shore.

Boats sliced the water on either side of my head, close enough I could smell the plugs of tobacco in the fishermen's cheeks. White foam strangled my song. I choked and retched but persevered singing, waiting for someone to hear my song and rescue me from my sunken perch on the Great Wall of the Ocean.

The fishermen ignored me, racing their boats through the lowered section of the Wall and throwing their nets into the mythic waters for the first time in ten years. Enormous fish flapped in their nets, catches the size of a fisherman's dreams.

A single ocean creature lent their ears to my song. The commanding red eye of the hungry sea beast softened and the tentacle wrapped around my leg loosened. Blood surged into my dead foot and the pins and needles pushed my singing voice into the highest register I've ever achieved.

Every soul returns to the sea, to be birthed anew
Netted fish surrender peacefully, because they know it's true
Next tide they'll cast the nets instead
Long after fishermen are dead
Just like lovers, we take turns feeding one another

I repeated the final line, turning it into a lullaby. The red eye relaxed and the tentacle released my leg. Music soothes the savage beast, I suppose. I was sorry when the eye disappeared under the water. I enjoyed their audience and had been prepared to give them a second song.

The stone cogs clanked again, and the Great Wall of the Ocean rose from the water. Confused shouts erupted from the fishing boats trapped on the other side. The voices soon turned to panic, what Uncle Lou would have called the first step on the path to disaster. As the Wall lifted me into the air, I cupped my hands to my mouth and shouted, "Give her a song!" It was worth a shot, but none of the fishermen heard me, too busy dooming themselves.

I pulled the dress over my head and left it on top of the Wall for the birds to pull apart for fresh nests. I didn't look back as the beast's many tentacles shot out of the ocean, grabbing boats by the stern and pulling them deep beneath the waves. Soon, the churning water filled with gnawed wood and the blood of three generations.

Free of my constrictive dress, I dove from the top of the Wall and swam for home. The entire village waited along the pier, fires stoked on the beach, expecting our fishermen to return with this decade's catch. Their nets should have carried enough to put an end to our hunger for the next few years.

The villagers were certainly surprised to see me crawl out of the water; half-drowned, singing of sunken ships and devoured men. Pits of salt were spread across the beach, ready to preserve the important catch. But thanks to me, there would be no end to our hunger tonight.

When I stood in the water with one foot beyond the wall, I imagined myself being commemorated for my rare feat. That sixteen-year-old girl's vanity turned out to be correct. Although exiled to the farthest edge of the island, I am certainly remembered. Every child learns the song about the wicked girl who refused her sacrifice and betrayed our starving fishermen.

The missing bones washed back ashore
Fruit of the sea beast bride's cruelty
She trapped many boats beyond the wall
Even the nets of her own family

...AND THE DEEP BLUE SEA

by Kerryn Elizabeth Salter

The smell of her sickness, salty and ripe,
Sea urchins and peaches
Fruit of the sea, and of Eden
(one supposes not only the apples were bad).
I had taken from her, then watched
As she was taken from me,
'til all that was left –
her skeletal resolve, ossified.
A sand dollar, a wooden stone.
Punished and pounded
then buried.
Saved? No, teased free by the tide
and left high upon the shore,
with a Devil's chance of ablution
or cure for her disease.

THE MOTH AND THE CANDLE

by Mike Anderson

I write this tale with my unaccustomed hand, for my other is broken and will be of no use for such things ever again; though, in truth, my sight of future needs has grown dim. The pen I clutch in cold-toughened fingers is a sharpened sliver of baleen; the ink is the sepia of the great cuttle, gathered from its very gut, and I write upon the stretched skin of the whale, cured in salt these last weeks.

This story must be told, and hope's joy of rescue grows fainter as the weeks pass. The sails I saw in the night will not return. I feel it. Nor should I expect them to, for what madman would steer a course to the south in this ultimate south sea, when the sting of winter mocks the burning cold of fall?

As nearly as I can figure, this is the seventeenth day of February in this Year of our Lord 1818, and fully six weeks since the terrible day when the beast came up and broke the fine ship *Seagull*—a New England whaler of seven hundred-ninety tons, out of the port of Martha's Vineyard.

Three years from home we were, via the South Seas to the great whaling grounds off Japan, and on to the empty seas where sperm whales rampage in the night to the west of Central America. Casks filled with the richest of all whale oils, holds bursting with ivory and spermaceti, and a chest filled with ambergris, every man aboard homecoming rich....

Those days seem far off now as I sit alone in this crude hut built of *Seagull's* crushed timbers and listen to the wind as it rocks the walls in their footings. My mind wanders and sometimes I lie for hours and see nothing, my tallow candle guttering low. Again, I must light a new one, and soon I shall make fresh candles from the bin of cold, tough whale fat. Cruel is the irony: I went to sea to make a wage from harvesting the whale and now I grub my most meager survival from half a corpse, which lies on the shale by the pounding sea.

But where are my manners? My name is John Ashby. I am a first generation New Englander, son of an English merchant turned Colonial, and born between the wars against the British. I grew up on the Vineyard and sea salt was my life's blood. The greatest of the sea trades boasted a thousand ships from New Bedford, the Vineyard, Nantucket and Boston, and I sailed my first voyage at the age of fourteen. My second voyage, I was harpooner on a round-the-world endeavor, and my third...is the one that will never end.

Harpooner of the second boat, I was, under Second Mate Castle. Mr. Castle was a fair man and a grand sailor. It is hard for me to speak of my shipmates, who lie dead beneath the sea, or in the row of graves outside—all but for Captain Garrett; and that devil I will curse until death takes me, for his madness sent us onto the fangs of stone and marooned me on the edge of the world.

When we first rounded the Horn, in the wind's eye on our way to the Pacific, we engaged a great-tailed demon. This male was seventy feet from the barrel of his head to the trails of his flukes, and he led us a dance for two days, with never an iron struck. Captain Garrett cursed the whale for bringing ill fortune upon the voyage so early, and from that moment forth he became withdrawn and sullen. He drove the crew hard and took to the boats himself on occasion, letting no spout go unchallenged.

In three years we had filled our casks and every cask the carpenters could build and sailed for home; but in the South Atlantic, near the place where the shorewise currents turn out to sea, we chanced upon a herd of lolling whales. And which beast should be among them, but the very demon that so tormented us before? The Captain seemed to lose his sanity and swore we would have one last killing.

This sorry tale is my story and cursed be the name of the greater devil who led us to our ruin.

❧❧❧

In his fortieth snow they sang of the strengths of Brandegyre,

Lord Chieftain of the Tribe and Clan of Throkrana. In the last days of summer, the People gathered in the warm currents where long swells broke above the mountains of the deep, to await his return. Young bulls thrashed the sea with the energy of youth. Brandegyre was their lord and master but one day, when age robbed him of strength, they would overthrow his rule and the cycle of change would begin anew.

He came out of the south—distant seas, the province of the Great Chiefs—and rejoined his clan in the yearly ritual of reunion. It was the way of life, the way life had always been, and would endure as long as whalekind. The urges of the season were hard upon him. He had little time for the sparring of his elder sons and dispatched their quarrelsome antics with sharp strokes of his flukes. As yet none would spar with him, jaw to jaw, for the right to claim the sultan's throne.

But into the foam-running seas, where the whales rolled and lolled under the sun, came a new and disturbing presence. A soft sighing of waters faded up in their range of hearing, and when Brandegyre lifted his head from the waves he saw the creation of men: creeping closer, blown on the wind, the mental stench of avarice strong and vile. He knew the stench, knew the single personality from which it emanated. Had he not outplayed this human, years ago? Now he perceived the purest hate—the guarantee of pursuit.

The bull Cachalot had long ago ceased to wonder at the predatory nature of men. They were but one more hostile thing in the ocean to be avoided, and he had learned the way in his forty snows. As the boats stood away from the parent craft and muffled oars drew near, Brandegyre sent the clan scattering and dived deep to evade the lances of the surface creatures.

Down in the echoing blue gloom, he studied the wooden craft. His sound waves passed through them and returned a ghostly, transparent image: organic shapes made of organic tissue, filled with creatures generating constant pulses on a narrow band. Deep in the parent craft, he sounded voids of air and other chambers full of *substances* which resonated with the same density as the bodies of whales.

He scowled mentally. There were tribes to whom hate was a stranger, but Cachalot was not one of them. Anger was as much his friend as joy. Sometimes it served a purpose, and fury blossomed easily when one had been hunted more times than memory recalled.

These surface-dwellers were clever: they knew the movements of whales well, and Brandegyre knew the People were in danger. He sent them away on a tangential course and showed his flukes to the hunters—dared them by staying on the surface. Two boats came for him; a third went for the tribe.

As the minutes passed Brandegyre realized this was not like all the times before. Now he perceived the unseen presence of the one whose will drove the hunt—the focal point of a sour, bitter evil which threatened his People to no good end. There was not even greed. Just hate.

Panic took the tribe in its thrall and Brandegyre cruised through the liquid sky, thinking quickly. He had known another chief, in the cold seas of the ultimate south, who fought back against his tormentors; and the time was surely right.

Now the anger was upon him. He snatched a breath before he turned toward the People and ran hard, leaving the two boats behind. The third was close to a pack of his mates, and their endurance was waning. He knew with awful dread, he would not be in time, and panic made them deaf to his commands. He heard and felt as an iron struck home. A young whale bucked in white pain, dived deep and took out the line. Brandegyre's anger swelled with the moment. He closed on the craft, saw the sonic echo of line dangling, whipping back and forth as the struck whale dived in panic while the others milled and cried out.

The surface creatures would never know what took their lives. Brandegyre rose beneath their craft, turned head-down and kicked his flukes. All the power of a tail twenty feet broad surged upward in an eruption of white water, sent splintered timbers, men and gear sky high. Coils of rope spilled into the sea with sails, goods and oars, a chaotic jumble which disappeared into the blue, drowning the cries of broken men.

Now, with only the last two boats to deal with, Brandegyre marshaled his people with the roar of authority and sent them north into the warm currents. The senior mates buoyed up the young whale who trailed the harpoon and now endless line. One of them would have it out later, with dextrous jaws—and the will of Providence.

Brandegyre knew a way to make the hunters lose interest in

his tribe. He faced them brazenly, spyhopped to look at them, then led them away from his receding folk. He could have played the game he had played years before — stayed beyond their reach until they tired — but now he wanted more. They had gone too far. Now they would pay.

As the boats came for him in the full passion of the chase he dived away, turned back and sped toward the parent craft. He sent an angry pulse toward it and perceived only a handful of creatures left within the vessel, which lumbered in the wake of its offspring. Brandegyre recalled the words of that other chieftain and steeled himself in his anger. He turned his blunt forehead to the wooden hull and rammed with all his strength.

He felt timbers groan and fibers snap, heard the clamor of fear from a dozen minds as he turned about and sank beneath the keel to batter it with his flukes, blow after blow. Slowly he realized, even as the assault injured him, he was succeeding.

The boats were returning. He stood away from the ship on the opposite side, let the land creatures swarm back to the fancied safety of their creation.

And then he breached, lofted his length from the water and fell back with a crash like thunder. He knew they saw him, knew they wanted his blood—and he knew their insensate rage would be their undoing: they could not imagine that the object of their ire had a fury which dwarfed their own to insignificance.

The cold eats into me and the wind never stops blowing. My mind wanders and I must force it back to the tale I tell....

Why the thrice-damned captain could not let it be was the question we all asked. We were rich and wanted only to sight New England to spend it. But there was still the element of greed, to which a stray spout appealed—the carpenters swore they could rig a few extra barrels where the reserve boat was stowed. Ships had made port in the past with bottles and jars hung in the rigging; who were we to turn down a final kill? *Greed.* The death of us all...and you who read this, take note.

We stood away. The grim old man was in the lead boat, and number three went to score a cow while we pulled hard for the demon fish; and as we went, so did our blood heat up. The thrill came back, and we saw our profits growing, but as the day progressed we learned the folly, the stupidity, of over-reaching oneself. Greed turned to anger, and anger to fear.

The beast sent eight men to their deaths and turned his evil upon the <u>Seagull</u>, and with all dispatch we pulled hard for home. What use is money if you're drowned dead? We forgot the devil as we stowed the boats, and hands took to the pumps while the officers inspected our wounded side. No timbers had parted, but the caulking was hurt and we were taking water as a result. Oakum fibers, hammered in, filled the spaces; within the hour we thanked God the level in the bilges was falling.

But what of the captain? Did he take his rebuke from the fish and go his way with a whole skin and a bulging money-belt? He knew not the meaning of such sense, and we found him standing in the bow, staring fixedly at the whale, which lay off our starboard side. They seemed to taunt each other, and all aboard knew we were headed wherever that creature would lead us...or to mutiny.

On recollecting that moment I cannot help feeling mutiny was the far wiser course of action. Ships come home without their captains on occasion, and this should have been one of them.

But no; we could not see the future clearly enough to tell the road we trod from the road we should have, so we followed orders, crammed on sail and steered a course for the great-tailed monster. As if possessed, Captain Garrett drove the ship without concern for aught but keeping the beast in sight.

Days and nights passed, and we found the whale each dawn, rising from the salt deeps and attracting our attention with a fearful launching from the waves. Many were the crosses made by sea-hardened hands; many were the fearful whisperings—that this beast was called up from places deeper than the ocean. Or else our captain was.

Twice, we lowered away to give chase; twice we spent fruitless days in bitter winds, longing for our hammocks as we played hide-and-seek with the giant. Never once did we reach striking distance, never once did it attack us. It would wait for us when we were exhausted, and numb hands fumbled with the davits to recover the boats...but always it was there, seeming to beckon, as if our journey was incomplete. The road to hell is long and paved with suffering.

We were going south once more — south, in the teeth of the coming winter, a fool's game without doubt. Yet there lingered the ghostly suspicion that a kill was but one launching away: and this whale was worth a fortune when he turned to oil in our trypots.

Onward, ever south, the cold creeping into our tired bodies. Fresh water was low since we had not taken on the brackish excuse for drinking water Central American ports had to offer, and we were at the end of our endurance for salt beef. Whale meat and hardtack alone remained, and the scrappy leavings in the fruit barrel.

We should have been raising the tropics off Brazil, with fresh food for the taking, but the monster led us on—lured us with a mixture of greed and the hate bred of effrontery at being out-thought by a fish. Surely, we thought, not much further. Already we were in the latitudes of the horn, and well to the east of it where the seas roll, gray and terrible, to the ends of the earth.

Stories passed dark hours in the foc'sle, told by drunken wretches who had survived the South Seas: stories of a world of ice where no living thing moved and the sea congealed, turned from water to white knives which could shear a ship apart with the ease of an angel's kiss. A world where the sun never set and monstrous birds with wings the span of a boat's length flew all their lives without a single beat. Of black and white whales more ferocious than sharks and strange, shadowy whales so huge, a ship could lie upon their backs without waking them. But every tale told of the cold, and the dreadful vision of a sea stretching around the bottom of the globe past unknown worlds of ice.

The day came we would take it no more, and the final foul day it was. For on this day the first motes of snow fell from black clouds. A lowering sun shone sickly yellow through racing thunder-rags, and we raised a jagged islet by the unholy glare of a spire of ice which seemed to grow from its crown. The monster that had led us disappeared then, and we hove to with a sudden pang of anticlimax. Had the creature brought us here just to vanish? Were we not to make one final kill?

Long we tacked against the endless west wind, circling the forbidding islet as stormheads soared above. Splayed fingers of light showed us where the sun must be. At times we could not look upon the mountain of ice, so brightly did it shine; even those of us ready to take the ship back from madness by force of arms were hushed by its awful majesty.

At last the waters broke whitely about a dark shape, and our blood was fired one last resolute, suicidal time. My hand shakes as I try to write this. I see in detail as we lowered away and pulled through the huge waves toward the shape in the sea, backed by the shining saw-edged mountain. I still feel the biting cold of the spray on our cracked, swollen faces, hear the wind that mocks mankind.

From the bow, harpoon in hand, I saw *Seagull* tacking after us with her handful of men, and with the weight of the world upon me I knew we would never see New England again.

⁂

On, through the darkness of the world in winter. The great Cachalot swam steadily, day after day, an ice-cold, calculating fury in his heart. He knew where he was going and what he would do when he got there. He could read the vibrations from the vessel which doggedly, stupidly, pursued him. He might have lost it with ease—taken a breath, submerged for over an hour and swum most of the way to the horizon in that time; but he wanted the humans where they were.

They could not molest his tribe if they were trying—and failing—to molest *him*. And when he was finished they would molest no one else ever again.

Brandegyre sensed the growing restiveness of the sea, as it answered the tug of the infinite easterly wind. The waves became steep and short. Strong echoes butted into the world-girdling groundswell. His destination was close now, and so long as the single-minded and rapacious predators would stick to him, he would show them the wages of their greed.

He heard the voices of other bulls, the last to leave these inhospitable waters before winter took hold, but he declined to follow them. Their ultra-fast sonic pulses rained in on him, asking, probing. They sensed the knot of hate coiled in him like a clenched fist, ready to strike when the moment was right; and they left him be. They all knew what he hunted. Many knew what it meant to fight back, and the fight had taken on the air of divine mission. Men and ships had been destroyed utterly before. They would be again. The war was far from one-sided.

There was no thought in Brandegyre's mind of failure; he became more certain as the strange creatures from the dry land stayed with him. And when at last, by the ghostly image of the world he perceived in his mind's eye, he knew the place was near, he left the ship momentarily.

He glided down into the cold, dark, heavy world of the watersky where the deep plains echoed to the murmurs of the ages. The world of whales was forbidden to men by the very laws of nature. Another lived down here, one he knew, and whose unwilling help he would enlist to spice his hate.

The cry froze in my throat as I raised the harpoon to cast, for the whale tossed and rolled madly upon the waves. In the darkness, its huge head seemed even more swollen than is usual for its kind. Something bristled, wriggled, lashed and, as the whale stood upon its tail in the momentary light of a sunray, we beheld the most hideous spectacle.

Clenched in the fifteen-foot jaw was a rubbery mass of flesh from which eyes shone with a balefire which stole the souls from our hearts. A gorgon's mane of reaching snakes thrashed the air, ravened at the whale's head, leaving weals of torn skin and blood.

For what seemed an age we were frozen by the sight; then the whale toppled like a falling iceberg. The horrible squid, lofted to the wan daylight, came down toward <u>us</u>. We pulled as if our hearts would burst, and the dueling monsters crashed down in a welter of foam which lifted us on a mound of black froth, up into the light before we plunged down once more into the chasm between the waves.

Mountainous bodies swelled up alongside and the longboat was cast over on her beams. Gear and men spilled over and we clung to the upper gunwale. My face was a foot from the black hide of our quarry before we righted with freezing water about our knees. Bailing desperately, we let the wind have us while we saw to our own lives, and by then we had no thought of taking on those unspeakable jaws again.

But the next awesome lurch of the titans upended the captain's boat, and it came apart as the squid, locked in the whale's jaws, hammered through it. The men were driven under as snake-like arms lashed around the captain, locked him to the whale's face. His harpoon was lost, and the timbers of the boat ravelled in a net and web of rope, sails and oars.

A tidal wave seemed to vomit from the deep and spat us up, broken and pummelled, on the shale beach of that grim isle. The last boat's keel ripped out as we spilled half-dead into the icy shallows, not ten yards from a scene that mocks the mind's imagination and words' ability to describe.

Torn loose from the whale by the shock of impact, the squid flailed and lashed on the shore. Boat timbers and cable wrapped it around and around into a gnarled fist of flesh—it flopped and whipped in inhuman frenzy.

Among it all the captain seemed woven in a tapestry of flotsam. One arm was pinned at his side, the other severed at the elbow and waving blindly as he shrieked his madness away. His broken body was broken again as the giant cuttle writhed its own life out, tentacles tearing at him while its own blood pooled on the shore.

In the darkness of the storm the whale watched from the breakers, head thrust up and lit in the false sunlight of the glaring mountain above us. As if some other man's hand accomplished the deed, I took up my own harpoon, which lay bent upon the shore. I stepped closer and, with bile in my throat, cast the iron true. To have cast at the whale would have been futile. I like to believe that in a moment of sanity I ended my captain's life and the squid's with the same razor thrust.

Seagull had observed our plight and ran downwind to our aid as the spare boat was unlimbered. As her sails hove into sight, shining white in the flash of the ice peak, the monster surged away into the swells, great tail cutting the waves. We poor handful from the one boat stood shuddering with fear as we foresaw what would happen.

Now the beast's fury made ours look puny, and we could only watch. With an impact that seemed great enough to end the world, the whale rammed the ship bows-on. Planking gave way under the stress of sail and titan; water rushed aboard as she faltered in her motion and the top yards carried away on the gale. High in the sky, sails flickered like clouds, not falling but blown out of sight, a tangle of rigging like a spider's web following in their train.

We saw <u>Seagull</u> heel as she was struck again, shudder as the whale battered the stern and sheered the rudder chains. Helpless and maimed, our only hope of living was driven ashore by the wind. Over the breakers we heard the thunderous scream as submerged rocks tore the life out of her, and the drum-beat blows as the whale struck again and again.

Setting these things down, I find I cannot hate the whale. Perhaps it is my delirium, but with human humbleness I acknowledge what it means to be the object of another's hate; to lose the fight and see another laugh.

Perhaps in his way the whale laughs at man, for when the terms are his, the lonely human is helpless. All the whales whose lives I have taken…I wonder if their kind grieves and remembers. I know they can hate, and I know the result of unleashing a demon.

Perhaps God has abandoned me, or perhaps He has privileged me alone to perceive a truth and set it down for those yet to come. I would hope the agony of the days since the beast cast us adrift here hold some purpose.

⚓⚓⚓

Revenge, the sweet nectar of the damned. Brandegyre drove the ship's broken ribs onto the rock shelf below the beach, forced the black stone fangs through his enemy's body. He knew he was ending the battle, calling the final halt to the evil which had stolen the lives of whales in so many seas.

He felt the chilling flood of oil and spermaceti from the ship's ruptured casks and backed away with a deep, unquenchable loathing. He returned to the quiet depths beyond the shelving margins of the island to ease his torn body. Fresh scars trailed blood into the night and sang their song of pain.

He knew survivors had reached the shore, but he knew they were beaten. Their mind-talk was a demented whisper on the edges of his perception and he closed it out, sank into the calm waters below the reach of the storm and rested. They would keep.

The processes of life repaired his flesh as days passed, and he hunted in the serene depths, taking the smaller squid which prowled in the cold void. Slowly his strength returned, and his tissues healed; the pain that had racked his head from the collisions inflicted upon the ship subsided. Pride and arrogant power settled, and peace slowly returned to his heart.

The surface dwellers had offended against the People—and against himself in no small measure—but he had exacted the price, and enough was enough. His tribe was waiting far to the north and he had wasted weeks already.

But he could not draw himself away from the glowing mountain, and would lie in the long rollers at dawn and dusk to see the ice shine like a hundred suns against the night sky. First the very tip, then a sheet of light as the rays inched down the face, or retreated to the summit with day's end. It mesmerized the Cachalot: a metaphor for the rise and fall of life in all its many cycles, tied implicitly to the arc of his lord, the Sun, upon whom all life depended.

He saw the fires of men on the wind-blasted slopes below the sheer ice face. The tiny lights seemed to confirm his concept of the worth of humankind, judged against the grandeur of the ocean world.

Slowly the mind-voices quietened and the fires grew fewer. One day, he knew, the fires would burn no more, and a strange sadness overset the final victory. The one from whom evil had shone like a black sun was gone. Brandegyre had flung the man onto the shore with the coiling bulk of his arch foe—felt the instant of their passing; and he had channeled the warm, spreading fulfilment into the final act when he smashed the ship, tore the humans' *thing* to pieces on the savage shoals.

As stars wheeled among raging auroras he sensed a welling burst of joy in the survivors and cast an eye upward, past the island. Its mountain shone redly below the fire in the heavens. He turned about to scan the dark waters and heard the faint patina of sound, which suggested a ship was butting against the waves. Sails were a snap and rustle of canvas somewhere far away; but it came no closer.

The end was the end, and deep down he took no pleasure in it. The days were short, the nights long; the ice was on the move, and the warm, bright world of the north beckoned him with the promise of love and peace. The great Cachalot put the hunt into the past, took in the mystic ice peak one last time, and set his course for the tropics.

Strive as he might to put sense to the uncalled-for predation of humans, he found no answer save greed—and it had become a fact of life for all whales. In the end there was no sense, and they lived their lives in the time the Sun saw fit to bestow upon them.

⁑⁂⁑

And so my story is almost told. Little is left to say but that we eight from the second boat watched our shipmates die as <u>Seagull</u> broke up and great pieces of her were driven ashore. We gathered what we could and took it well above the shore, to a windy place where we could see to the forbidding horizons. We made fire with the ship's bones, to drive out the cold which was killing us.

Snow fell the first night and we sheltered under the remains of the longboat, which we dragged to high ground and covered with the sail from its locker, rigged with line hacked from the drifting jumble. We burned wood, which jostled ashore, fired with the pure whale oil…the cause of our whole misery…from an unbroken barrel found rolling on the shale. It meant our very lives, as it kept the snow from killing us as we huddled over the flames in soaked leather and woollen clothes, and the wind shook the sailcloth like an angry fist.

When the sun rose, yellow and dim, from out a churning sea we found ourselves weak and ill with the numbness of cold and sheer hopelessness. We kept the fire burning in the lee of the boat with timber dipped in oil, and dried ourselves as best we could before braving the wind to gather our belongings.

It happened that our boat's provisions had survived, and we had a few days' supply of salt meat, biscuit and fresh water. With this fare we knew we had a chance, and so began the heartbreaking task of sorting *Seagull's* remains for the timbers, lines and makeshift tools with which to build a proper shelter.

It was hard and filthy work, but sailors are not unused to the labor. It took the whole day to drag the lumber to high ground, use what ironworks survived to tear a foundation from the stony earth and repack it to hold up the slabs and frames of wood. At last the gaps were filled with sailcloth and we secured a roof of plank, woven together with rope. Inside, a fire soon warmed the air and we ate our meat hot.

But the work served only to conceal the fact there was no point to the labor. We had shelter, but soon we would starve. And some of us would die. Pneumonia took us one by one, a gentle madness as we froze and the wind raged on. The line of stone cairns began to lengthen. A man took a fall to the shale beach and passed away before we could help him. Another was twisted with pains and coughed red blood.

It seemed I alone stayed reasonably fit until the day I broke my hand, falling with it beneath me. Mr. Castle pulled it straight and bound it tightly, but it has hardly moved since and the pain is a blank place in my memory. Then came the day I was alone. I buried my last comrade and wished to die as well.

I thought to walk into the sea and let the monster have me, but the bay where the squid lies is a place of evil memories, and I trudged another way. It was then I came upon the lone and rigid carcass of a whale upon the beach—a *mysticeti* of one sort or another, old and blackened. I took from it the fat, meat and other materials upon which survival might depend. The thought was at once in my mind…I may set down what has transpired, so at least my story might stand in testimony of the last voyage of the *Seagull*.

We saw sails in the darkness, or thought we did. For a while the sighting buoyed the spirits of the few who remained, but the ship passed as it came. One thing I recall: when I walked out upon the rocky headland the titan was there below, watching me. I felt like a caged prisoner, my unholy jailer prowling in the shadows. It would rise up and look at me, yet after all that had gone before—after all we had done to kill each other—we no longer looked upon each other with mutual hate.

Sometimes in the long hours, ghosts come out of the line of cairns to speak to me, their tired voices a babble of silent sounds. I cannot understand. It is as if they now know a great thing, and it is I who am ignorant. The Book of Job says of the whale, he is the holder of all high things; and with this in mind I ask myself why we hunt so blessed a beast. Perhaps this is the answer I seek.

Men hold ourselves in such wonderful esteem—such magnified importance over our fellow creatures. But my mind draws the hurtful picture: if there were flying things here, a moth would surely flutter to my candle, so fascinated by the living light that it cannot resist drawing nearer until it touches the flame and is gone.

Is this not the way we came to this speck of land at the end of the world? Drawn on by our awful obsession with phantom wealth, and with a desire to prove ourselves superior to the animal we pursued, at last we showed ourselves more synonymous with the moth. We touched the flame, and we are gone.

Sailing home rich was what we wanted, but there is some spark in man that cannot leave alone what he clearly does not comprehend. It is too late now for me to know, not all whales are equal; or that I saw in the leviathan a human-like drive and will, a man's anger…or that I can indeed respect the monster—and not merely because I shall be at its mercy if I once more stray upon the waters. These things have meaning to me only because of who I am; to all the other untold folks in the world they would be the ravings of a lunatic.

Some days ago, the beast vanished. I have looked long but I see no spout pacing the waters offshore. Now I am truly alone with the wind, my thoughts and this tale; and for all its menace, I somehow miss my terrible companion.

I have set down these words with all the truth I can manage, though my memory is not the best and I can write so little each day. A meal of thawed whale meat and a few pieces of sea greens, from where the tide is low, are barely enough to keep body and soul together, and in truth I do not know that it matters one way or t'other.

The days are very short now and the snows come more often. The mountain groans and moves sometimes, with a sound louder than a cannon-shot. Come what may, I am at the end. I live without purpose. If the ship we saw comes back, I shall speak to men once more. And if it does not....this tale shall speak for me.

FINWIFE

by Carmen Fowle

Carmen Fowle

Arabella tensed as a knock sounded at her door; she'd long expected the sound, yet had hoped not to hear it.

"Come in," she called, shoulders slumping as she leaned against the wooden panels lining the small window seat. Her gaze remained fixed upon the sea as it rippled, swirled, and waved from the other side of the glass. It was calm today, and she could easily lose herself within the patterns as they danced across her vision. A week ago, such sights would have sent her cowering into windowless rooms, but she'd since found the beauty in them, even granting herself permission to admire them.

Music and chatter drifted in from the ballroom as the door to her chambers opened and closed again, the music replaced by the much softer beat of footsteps crossing the room. Clearly the festivities were well underway, and her absence had been noted.

"Uncle," she greeted without turning to look. "I'm sorry, I—" Her attempt at apology and excuse were silenced by a light rustle of fabrics and presence of a hand upon her cheek, gently coaxing her to turn away from the glass.

"What is it, Bell?" Her uncle's voice was soft as she followed his guidance, turning to look at him as he crouched beside her without a care for the wrinkles that would surely mar his crisp formal attire.

Arabella looked at him, grateful for the lack of reprimand, but unable to find the words. "It's... I'm... We're..." she stuttered, trying again and again to convey her thoughts. Finally, she sighed and settled on "I looked on Papa's globe." Her gaze flicked back towards the window as she gave a little nod towards it. "We're about... where they were." Her lower lip trembled, and she bit down on it in a most unladylike manner. She couldn't bear to finish her thought, to make her parents' recent death into a reality. Not yet.

Arabella's uncle was still for a moment, then gave a slow nod as he gently squeezed her hand. "I'm so sorry, Bell," he whispered the words, his own gaze distant as he peered towards the window. "I hadn't thought."

Arabella only shrugged. The planned route wasn't within her uncle's power to change, nor was it something she'd expected him to fully consider. Besides, any course alterations would've significantly increased the duration of the voyage. All she really wanted was to arrive at her new home and allow herself to grieve.

Though she was of age, her parents' wills had requested she remain under the guardianship of her uncle Royce until she married. Arabella had been all too happy to agree, not wishing to be alone in her childhood home. Of course, that meant *leaving* her childhood home and traversing the dreaded sea to Royce's household. She'd examined the globe before they left, curious about the path. They wouldn't stop in Orkney, but they *would* sail close enough to glimpse it by eye. Now they were nearly halfway through their journey, she could just barely see it off in the distance, growing ever closer with each gentle wave that rocked the ship.

"I'm sure everyone will understand if you don't wish to attend the festivities," Royce broke the silence. "I could have a meal sent for you."

Arabella shook her head. "I'll make an appearance soon," she promised. "I just want to sit a little longer." In truth, she'd been looking forward to the mid-voyage masquerade as a means of distracting herself from reality, if only for a few hours. She'd tried to remain friendly and pleasant in her interactions with the other passengers during the voyage so far: she'd carefully avoided the topics she wished to remain hidden, but somehow it had slipped out and made the rounds. Now it seemed she couldn't go longer than a few moments in public without someone offering condolences or treating her as a damaged gemstone, ready to shatter under even the lightest of pressure. The masquerade would take some of that away, offering a reprieve from the sympathies as she hid her face behind a mask. She knew she was likely to be identified by other means, but the chance to breathe and be herself—if only for a moment—was enough to sway her.

"Would you like an escort?"

Arabella shook her head again. "I'd rather not draw attention to myself. But thank you for the offer." A warm smile graced her face for the first time since she'd heard the news, sincerely grateful. Though they'd suffered a bit of a rocky start, her uncle showed a certain kindness that made her confident their arrangement would work. She would be ok. They would look after each other. Together, they would get through this.

"Very well," Royce returned her smile, giving her hand another gentle squeeze. "I'll see you whenever you're ready, then." He released her hand, grunting softly as he rose from his crouch. He watched her a moment longer, then gave a deep nod of farewell.

Arabella returned his nod, once more turning to seas beyond the window, though she'd barely focused as Royce spoke once more.

"Try to enjoy yourself, Bell, if only a little," he stood near the doorway, smiling as he slid his mask over his face, the intricate design of colours and gemstones sparkling as they caught the light. "You deserve an evening of happiness."

"Thank you, Uncle." The words didn't seem enough to express her sentiment, but they would have to do.

☙ ☙ ☙

Arabella waited until dusk before joining the festivities, lingering until she could no longer see the approaching islands from her window. She'd slipped into the grand hall, using a side entrance rather than the main to avoid drawing attention. Royce had caught her eye and given her a quick nod and smile, though left her to her own devices. He was nearby if she needed him, she knew, though she hoped not to require such aid.

The evening wore on quickly, but Arabella found she enjoyed herself a good deal more than she'd expected to. The food—thankfully still making the rounds—was delicious, and the company was even better. If anyone recognized her, they hadn't revealed it; it seemed everyone was under silent agreement to abide by the anonymity provided by the masks.

She'd danced with many young men, some out of courtesy, others for the conversation. She'd often felt Royce's gaze on her as she'd danced, likely quietly judging her partner's suitability for courtship. He'd refrained from stepping in, from relieving her of any partners, though she *had* caught him giving a subtle shake of the head once or twice. Fine by her—she wasn't actively seeking courtship at the moment. Even if she were, she hadn't found those particular gentlemen to be of interest.

"Might I have the next dance, my lady?" A deep, strangely accented voice posed the question, its owner extending a deeply tanned hand to her as he swept into a rather stiff and awkward bow.

Arabella set her hand in his, silently accepting the offer as she bid her previous partner farewell. The poor man couldn't seem to leave quick enough, clearly having cared for her company as much as she'd enjoyed his. No loss, she supposed, turning her attention towards the newcomer as the song began.

They danced in silence for a few moments, allowing Arabella a chance to better examine her new partner. He stood a head or so taller than her, but it was his clothing that drew her eye. His vibrant yellow-green drapings were loose and flowing around his thin frame, swaying with each movement as he carefully twirled her about. Compared to the form fitting dark attire the other men sported, he stuck out like a beacon in the dark, and she wondered how she'd not caught sight of him before now.

The song slowed, and he pulled her closer, bending a little, until his chin brushed against her shoulder. "It's lovely to see you enjoying yourself, Lady Arabella." His breath tickled her ear as he directed his soft words towards it.

Arabella gasped, pulling back, searching the eyes behind his ornate starfish shaped mask. His was a voice she was sure she'd recall, yet she had no memory of it. Nor did his eyes strike her as familiar. Had she met this man before?

"Are you well, my lady?" The man in the starfish mask had ceased dancing, watching her.

Royce caught her eye from his own dance nearby, head quirked to the side in silent question.

Arabella shook her head, simultaneously shaking the thoughts from her mind and attempting to reassure her uncle. "Quite well, thank you," she turned and offered a smile to her uniquely clad companion. "Though I could use some air. I wonder if you might like to escort me?" She was fairly certain she'd just broken a few rules of polite society, but decorum be damned—she needed a quieter place to think.

"It would be my honour." Her companion held his arm out to her, and she took it, allowing him to escort her out on deck and down the walkway with the best views of the passing scenery. It was as if he'd known she hoped for another glimpse of the Orkney Islands as they passed them.

"Forgive me," Arabella broke the silence as the music faded behind them, "but I seem to have forgotten your name."

"Marsious," her companion offered with a smile. "I hold no fault against you. It's not a common name." He seemed much more relaxed, now they were away from the crowds.

An understatement to say the least; Arabella was positive she'd never heard such a name before. Just as she was quite certain she'd not heard his voice before, nor seen those mirthless eyes. Yet he'd known who she was, as if they'd met before. There had to be something she'd not considered, something she'd forgotten, some logical explanation.

Any concern she felt for the matter was fleeting, however, her mind distracted as they paused by the rail. A shiver ran through her as she saw the familiar outlines of the islands she'd been dutifully watching all afternoon. They were closer than ever, likely as close as they would come. She wished they could have passed by in the daylight.

Marsious put an arm around her bare shoulders, shielding her from the light breeze, misinterpreting the shiver.

"Thank you." Arabella didn't have the heart to correct him.

"The winds are always chilled here," Marsious gestured toward the island in front of them with his free hand. "Though it's quite pleasant in the midsummer heat."

"You're familiar with Orkney?" Arabella looked to her new companion in surprise.

"I am," Marsious gave a single nod, gaze still fixed ahead. "I grew up there." There was pride in his voice, though it was gone as soon as it came. "Have you visited?"

"No." The response came sharper than Arabella had intended. "My parents have, but…" Just how much could she trust this man? Hadn't she hoped to avoid such conversations for the night? Still, she'd said so much already… "Sadly they also perished there. Lost at sea during a fishing excursion." At least, that's what the official reports said. The officer who'd come to bear the news had seemed hesitant and secretive, refusing to answer questions. Royce had later admitted there'd been no signs of her parents' bodies, but the small fishing boat they'd borrowed for the day had washed ashore as timbers. Odd that they'd been out on a fishing voyage at all, considering her mother's fear of what lurked within the depths, though it wouldn't be the first time she'd relented and agreed to partake in her husband's hobby. "Quite recently, actually." Her gaze swept over the little bit of shoreline that shimmered like gold in the moonlight, secretly wishing to see her parents there, alive and well, perhaps even pausing to wave at the ship as it sailed past. Though her mother had disliked traveling by boat, she'd always happily waved at them from the shore.

"I'm very sorry to hear it," Marsious' words sounded sincere enough, though Arabella didn't miss the tightening of his hand on her shoulder, nor the almost possessive way he pulled her closer. "Was it one of the Finfolk? They tend to be rather territorial, especially when it comes to fishing grounds."

Arabella blinked at him, unsure how to feel about his words. According to Royce, the Finfolk had been the very same creatures some of the locals had blamed for her parents' disappearance. And yet…

"I'm a little old for fairy tales, Marsious."

"Or in this case, fish tails," Marsious chuckled heartily, though ceased as Arabella failed to join him. "Apologies. A joke in poor taste." He held a hand over his heart as he spoke the sentiment.

Arabella frowned, not wishing to hear anything more about the mythical creatures, or jokes about them. She looked up at the moon in the sky, then back to Marsious. "It's late. I think perhaps I ought to retire for the evening."

"I hope I did not offend, my lady—"

"No, no!" Arabella wasn't yet sure if she spoke the truth. She didn't care for his belief in myths and legends, but had enjoyed his company enough that she felt he deserved a second chance. "I'm very glad for the dance, and the walk," she smiled. "Perhaps we can speak more during another."

"I look forward to it." Though he smiled again, the dark orbs behind his mask retained their deep-rooted sadness. What torments had he suffered to cause such a reaction? She wanted to ask, but wasn't sure she wished to know.

"Would you care for an escort back to your chambers?"

"Another time, perhaps." Arabella didn't miss the slip of Marsious' smile into frown. "I wish to find my uncle and bid him goodnight first." She'd felt him watching as she'd left the hall with Marsious, sensed the unease within him. She hated to be the cause of his worry.

"Until then, my lady," Marsious slowly—almost reluctantly—removed his arm from her shoulders, a mysterious glint flashing in his eyes, so fleeting she thought she may have imagined it. "I thank you for the lovely evening." He swept into another awkward bow and gently kissed her knuckle. His grasp remained steady and firm, though he allowed her hand to slip free as he slowly stepped away.

"Thank you, Marsious," Arabella remembered her manners, giving a little curtsey of her own before turning and venturing back the way they'd come. She looked back only once, surprised to see Marsious continuing along the path they'd been taking. He too glanced over his shoulder, smiling as he saw her watching him.

"Arabella? Are you—"

Royce's concerned tone drew Arabella's attention, and she stopped just short of having her uncle run into her, taking a small step back to avoid being knocked to the ground.

"Bell! Oh, thank goodness, I was worried!" Royce threw his arms around her, hugging her close, even as she stumbled into the rails behind her. He wasn't acting himself at all.

"I wasn't gone *that* long, Uncle," Arabella gripped the rail as she chuckled softly, suddenly glad her uncle had no children of his own. If this is how he reacted to her—a grown woman—venturing off on her own for a short time, she hated to think how he'd react to childish antics. He'd probably never sleep. "And I'm fine. Marsious was the perfect gentleman."

"You wouldn't believe the things others were saying about your companion," Royce seemed not to have heard her. "Bell, I'm not sure I'm comfortable with—"

A particularly large wave hit the ship, offsetting the both of them. Arabella tightened her grip on the rail, Royce quickly grabbing hold beside her. There wasn't a cloud in the sky, let alone sign of a storm—it was a beautiful night and the sea had been perfectly calm a moment ago. Yet the ship now rolled precariously within the waves, much like a toddler galloping on a rocking horse: upwards to a dangerous height, then crashing back down, water flooding the deck. Screams could be heard from within the much safer confines of the interior rooms, intermixed with shouts from the crew. None seemed to know what to do, aside from hanging on for dear life.

As the ship swooped upwards again, Arabella thought she saw something in the water. Something that seemed much too large to be a fish. Something that seemed to pause and look at her with all too familiar eyes, adding a splash of vibrant colour to the murky blue depths. But she blinked and it was gone. Her mind had to be playing tricks on her.

They plunged back towards the sea, hitting hard, knocking the wind from Arabella. She gasped for air, instinctively releasing her hold on the rail. She realized her mistake almost instantly.

"Bell!"

Arabella barely had time to register her uncle's shout as she was pulled down by the current. Frantic limbs stretched out towards her, and she fought to catch one; just one to pull her back to safety. But the ship rocked upwards again, swiftly dragging the limbs away from her, sending her further into the depths.

She thrashed against the watery turmoil, willing herself to rise, craving the air above. So close, yet so far… The tip of her nose rose above the waves—just a little more!

She surfaced, sputtering, drawing air deep into her lungs. "Help!" She slipped under, desperately fighting her way back up, once more calling for aid as she drew another breath, never in her life so glad to hear shouts returned.

Something wrapped around her ankle, jolting her downwards at a much quicker pace than before. She'd been mid-scream. Water filled her lungs where there should have been air. She kicked frantically, using every last ounce of strength to free herself. The offending anklet only tightened.

The world was growing darker, her vision blurring. Memories flashed before her eyes. Her mother lulling her to sleep with her lovely voice—she could almost hear it now, as a siren song. Her father reading to her on the swing in the backyard, beneath her favourite tree. Serving as bridesmaid at her friend's wedding, dodging the groomsman intent upon winning her heart. Her father dutifully holding her mother in his arms as they'd waved farewell for the last time. Royce escorting her onto the ship in much the same manner, whispering encouragement with each hesitant step she took…

Her mother's fears of the sea seemed so valid now. How had she ever come to find beauty in the waves?

Drawing one last gulp of water into her lungs, she felt the pressure surrounding her ankle release, quickly replaced by what felt like an arm around her waist. She thought she heard a whisper in her ear, but whatever slim amount of logic lingered in her mind reminded her that such a thing was impossible.

The world went dark.

❦❦❦

Arabella rolled over, coughing violently, sending copious amounts of water splashing across the sand beside her. She released one last lungful of water and breathed deep, savouring the sweet air.

Sand.

She was laying in sand.

Beneath the warm sun.

With oxygen in her lungs.

Alive.

She was alive.

The realization knocked her back towards the precious sand, landing so hard she nearly deprived herself of the air she'd come to love so much.

"Easy." The commanding voice was deep and familiar, nagging at the edge of her mind like a familiar song that had been played one too many times.

"Marsious." Arabella's voice was scratchy, like the sand she still couldn't believe she was laying in. "What—"

"I drowned you," Marsious' tone was nonchalant as he carefully removed the mask from her face. "Then I saved you." He examined the intricately painted silver mask, seemingly entranced by it.

"You *WHAT?*" Arabella winced, the utterance scalding her throat.

Marsious gave another shrug. "I wanted you, I took you," he

gestured to the land around him. "That's what the Finfolk *do*." He tucked her mask into a bag worn at his hip, giving it a little pat. "That and hoard silver. Of which I have quite the supply, I might add." He spoke as if she should be impressed, but she felt sickened.

Arabella sat up again, staring at him in horror. There was no such thing as Finfolk; it was all fairy stories. A myth. Not logic.

And yet, as she stared at him now, she saw it. What she'd taken for intricate drapings of cloth were actually… fins. The starfish piece he'd worn as a mask now sat atop his head as a coronet.

Not stories, no myth. Truth.

Her mouth fell open, the shriek dying in her throat.

"It's a pity, really," Marsious continued. "I *did* try to warn you."

Arabella barely heard a word he spoke. "Are my parents alive?"

Marsious shook his head. "Alas, I battered their boat just a tad too much." He chuckled, clearly incredibly proud of himself, without a shred of remorse. "Pity, really. They spoke very highly of you, and would have made such lovely additions to our little society. My brother Leomaris had wanted to claim your mother, though he didn't reach her in time." He allowed a chuckle, though Arabella saw little mirth in the situation he described. "I meant what I said about being territorial," his eyes darkened, his brow furrowing as he looked at her. "*Never* cross me, Arabella."

Arabella found it difficult to breathe, as if she were drowning all over again. She felt dizzy. "I wish to go home."

"You *are* home," All trace of the darkness left Marsious' face as he trailed a finger along her jaw, gesturing once more to the land around them with the other hand. "The Isle of Hildaland is where you shall stay until you've made the transformation."

Arabella glanced around, already plotting her escape. Where there was a beach, there was water. If she could find a boat… or create a signal of some sort?

"There is no escape from Hildaland," Marsious smirked, as though reading her thoughts. "No human save those upon it can see it, and you'd never get further than the shore before we retrieved you." He chuckled gleefully. "You may've noticed, we're quick swimmers."

She stared at him dumbly, not knowing what to say. Not able to process what *he* was saying.

"Fret not," Marsious' touch lingered at her cheek, giving it a gentle pat of comfort. "I shall remain with you for the summer, and you'll have plenty of company during the winter. Other humans like you, awaiting the day you can safely join us in our undersea haven." He leaned forwards, pressing a kiss to her forehead, as if that would speed whatever transformation he spoke of. "The day you shall live by my side as my beautiful Finwife."

THE GOD-SENT

by Soumya Sundar Mukherjee

Biru had seen the new man on the beach last night and guessed that this man must be the latest gift from the god.

But he had made no attempt to talk to the man; he just could not muster the courage. So, he went to his mother and told her what he had seen. His mother was, of course, happy, and she thanked the god and spread the news in the locality.

By the next evening, all men and women of the little sea-side village knew that the god had sent a gift. The little ones faced the sea and chanted the prayer "The god is good to us" before going to bed, as instructed by their parents.

The male members of the families gathered in 'Seagull Pub' to discuss the matter that evening.

Rajan said, "My wife told me that it has happened again."

Anuj said, "Yea, I heard that too. So, this year fishing will be good."

The barman, Vinit, said, "And so will be business. No rough wind or crashing waves this year, I hope. The sea good, we do well. The sea unhappy, trouble for us."

Rajan asked, "Who has seen him first? I mean, on the beach?"

Nitin, a man in his forties, proudly said, "That's my son, Biru. So, I'll have the honour to arrange for the boat."

Several of them watched him with envy. Someone murmured, "Lucky chap!"

Suddenly, Vinit the barman, cleared his throat and the whole crowd looked behind to see the man who was entering the pub.

The man looked at his surroundings with disdain, as if nothing in this place could match with his finer taste. He had the smile of a man who showed the fake helplessness of being among a bunch of rustic morons.

He came and sat on a stool and ordered a beer. He felt that

people were staring at him, *but that must be because this awful lot seldom see a man from the city, or the civilized parts of the country.*

Nitin said, "You seem to be new here, sir."

"Yes, I am." The man looked over his beer. "And I don't think I can stay here much longer."

The barman asked, "Why, Sir?"

"Not my type of place, you know. Too much dirt, too many dumb faces."

The village-folk looked at each other. *Is this man really the god-sent one?*

Rajan asked, "So, where are you coming from, Sir?"

The man suddenly seemed to be on guard. "I'm from the city, but that is none of your business."

Rajan swallowed and concentrated on his own drink.

The other men moved a little further from this arrogant person and began conversing among themselves. Anuj said, "I think he is the one. He *is* the man sent by the god of the great depths. He *has* every right to be impolite to us."

Rajan said, "But remember, 'impolite' does not always mean 'god-sent'.

Nitin said, "I think we should wait a little. If the god of the great depths has sent him, he will show us signs."

In the meantime, the barman was talking in a hushed voice with the new guest. The other men looked at the scene. They knew that Vinit would tell them all about it.

The man left. The village-folk surrounded the barman.

"Who is he, Vinit?"

"Where is he staying?"

"What was he asking you?"

"Is he really…?"

Vinit, the barman, looked a little confused. "Yea, I think this is our man. He is from the cities, and he is staying here in old Mohit's house near the light house. And he asked me where he could buy some *entertainment*, if you know what I mean."

All the men sniggered.

"The god has sent us really a good one this time, I see," said Nitin. "What did you answer him?"

The barman smiled. "I politely told him that there is no whorehouse in our village."

※ ※ ※

The man from the city had taken shelter in the house of old Mohit who lived with his young daughter Rina. Rina was beautiful, sweet and eighteen. Such qualities are hardly overlooked by bad men.

That night old Mohit was out for a stroll when he met a number of village people on the beach. When they asked him about his new guest, he said, "Yes, he could be the one, I've guessed it too. But he will show us signs; he will do something by which we can unmistakably understand that he is the god-sent one."

Rajan said, "If you don't mind, you have left Rina alone with the god-sent one?"

Mohit smiled, "Thanks for your concern, boy. But my girl knows a bit of self-defence. What about you? Who's going to arrange for the boats?"

"That's me, Uncle Mohit. My son saw him first on the beach," Nitin said.

Suddenly a flash of a torchlight made them stop in their path. A man in his mid-thirties came through the sand and joined them. "Who among you is Mohit? The barman from the Seagull Pub said that he can be found here, near the light house."

Old Mohit said, "I am Mohit. Who are you?"

"Glad to meet you," The man shook hands with him. "I am Detective Pande and I am searching for a criminal responsible for seven murders and two rapes. He is reported to have come to these parts. I heard from the barman that you have a guest who is new to this place. Can you have a look at this photograph and tell me whether you have met him or not?"

He took out a photograph from his pocket and shined his torch over it. All the men leaned forward to have a look at it. Then they looked at each other's eyes.

"No, Detective," said old Mohit without even a slight quiver in his voice. "Never seen him."

All the others nodded in consent. "Yea, yea, never seen a face like that around here."

"And your new guest?" The detective still tried to cling to a faint hope. "What about him?"

"He is my brother's son from the city," Mohit said lightly. "He

61

is an engineer. He is not your man, Detective."

Detective Pande observed all the faces surrounding him but could not find a valid reason for which all of these men would lie to him. He bowed a little to the company and went back.

This time the men watched him go and get into his car. The headlights shone as the man drove towards the city.

"An engineer, huh?" Nitin laughed.

All the others laughed with him. Rajan said, "Two rapes, seven murders. Yes, he is the god-sent, indeed. They are usually people with histories."

The men walked towards the residence of old Mohit which was near the light house. When they reached there, Mohit's daughter Rina was waiting for them at the front door.

⚜⚜⚜

Her blouse was torn at the left shoulder, her face and neck had scratch marks, her cheeks had marks of dry tears, her face was wild with uncontrollable frenzy.

She said in a hoarse voice, "He tried to take my virginity, father."

"And?" Old Mohit asked calmly.

"And he is now lying unconscious in the attic. I hit him on the head with one of your bottles.

"This confirms it," old Mohit nodded at the group.

"That's great news." The men were ecstatic. "Let's find some rope, gentlemen," said Rajan.

After fifteen minutes, they gathered again at Old Mohit's door to bid goodnight to each other. They had a big day coming.

"In my shop, I still have some brand-new binoculars left. Get one, if you don't have one." Anuj announced.

All the men walked to the dark sea and knelt on the beach. They took a handful of wet sand and reverently said, "We thank you, O the god of the great depths, for everything."

⚜⚜⚜

The next morning was one of festivity. The whole of the village was celebrating and waiting eagerly for the twilight.

62

Many of them had occupied seats at the light house. They were prepared with the binoculars. They looked at the brilliant dazzle of the sunlight over the thrashing waves. They looked at their watches and waited.

Nitin, Biru's father, was busy with the boats. He was proud that he had the opportunity to prepare the boats.

Then the sun began his westward journey from the zenith. They brought out the man from the city tightly bound with ropes.

The man was naked; upon his body they poured edible oil and fragrance. He could not make a sound; he was gagged up.

Then he was loaded upon the boat beautifully decorated by Nitin and this boat had been hooked up with a strong rope with Nitin's own fishing boat. Then Nitin, Biru and two other men from the village accompanied him to the wide sea. The whole of the village cheered behind them.

The salty wind greeted the two boats to the vast expansion of dark copper water of the sunset. They covered half a mile from the shore and stopped.

The enormity of the dark depths seemed to be so engulfing this time that even a veteran fisherman like Nitin felt a certain chill tingling in his spine. *Inside this rippling surface, lies the ....*

"Hurry up, boys!" Nitin shouted over the wind. "The sun is getting low. We should not be here when *he* comes."

They hastily unhooked the boat into which the Gift was lying wide awake, though unable to move. The Gift was staring at the darkening sky.

The fishing boat of Nitin let the Gift boat float over the waves. The people watching from the light house with the binoculars had a clearer view than most of the others. Old Mohit's daughter Rina was giving a running commentary to others: "Now they have released the Gift. …They are coming back. The Gift is moving towards the west where the water looks like blood. …Brother Nitin and his boat have arrived. The boat of the Gift is floating more to the west. …And Oh! Oh! Look! *He* is coming!"

The sea churned as if something massive was coming up to the surface. Those with powerful binoculars could even see the dark gigantic shape moving slowly under the glittering waves of the sunset and the boat was dancing toward it over the floating foams.

Then a long, sharp tentacle shot into the sky from under the water and smashed onto the Gift boat like a whip, causing it shatter like fragile china. Those into the light house could have the momentary glimpse of their divinity and they wept like children. Some of them even had convulsions at this grand spectacle of divine power. The Gift" vanished underwater without a trace.

The sun had set. The dark waters were calm. Nothing moved upon the surface anymore.

The villagers praised their god for his mercy and celebrated all night long.

OLLIE

by Ingrid L. Taylor

Mylie cowered in her bedroom closet, hands clamped over her ears, trying to drown out the shouting. Glass shattered as a body hit the wall. The smack of a fist on flesh echoed and she shrank deeper into the recesses, building a cocoon of downy jackets and bright scarves around her. She wished Jake was there. She always felt safer when he was around, but her brother was sixteen and had friends that could drive. He spent more and more time out of the house.

A door slammed. In the silence that followed, Mylie heard her mother crying. She could picture her mother as clearly as if she were downstairs with her. Her subdued weeping would gradually calm to soft gasps, as she lay, eyes closed, gathering energy. Then she would heave herself to her feet, wipe her face, and clean up the mess. It was a scene that had played out over and over for as long as Mylie could remember.

When she was younger, Mylie had rushed out of whatever hiding spot she had crawled into, suctioning to her mother as soon as the fight was over. Her face lined with pain, her mother would try to pull Mylie's clinging arms from her body.

Now that Mylie was older, she had learned to wait until the flood of tears subsided. Only then would she go to her mother and silently hold open the trash bag, wipe up spilled food, or whatever else was required to reassemble the illusion. Each time they repeated the charade, a piece of her insides scuttled off somewhere to die.

She pushed the closet door open and surveyed the dim room. Stuffed toys sat in rows on the bed and cheerful posters of animals and birds lined the pink walls. A jumble of books overflowed from a matching pastel bookshelf.

She looked up and down the hallway. The door to Jake's bedroom was closed. The last time they spent a day together was on her tenth birthday. He had taken her to the town aquarium, her favorite place in the world. She loved the soothing blue of the tanks, the easy grace of fish sliding through water. Her favorite exhibit held the resident octopus, Ollie. The first time she saw the bulbous eyes and writhing limbs, she never wanted to leave. Ollie had followed her as she walked back and forth in front of the tank. His body stretched and flattened to mold with his surroundings, unbound by shape or definition. His tentacles danced through the green water, breaking all the rules of movement that Mylie understood. A thrill vibrated inside her as she watched him. When he flashed his beak and twisted his large round head, Mylie sensed deep secrets passing between them. Even the promise of ice cream or a souvenir from the gift shop couldn't cajole her away as she flattened her palms on the aquarium glass, wishing she could float free with him in the water.

On her last visit with Jake, she had rushed to the octopus exhibit. Instead of Ollie greeting her with his soft purple shimmer, harsh white bulbs lit a barren tank. Jake read the sign posted next to the exhibit. Ollie had died.

Mylie had sunk to the floor, a shiver in her body and the feeling of ice wrapping around her heart. Jake had glanced at the dark shapes wandering past them. A young mother dragged along two small children, her gaze lingering on Mylie.

"Hey, get up. People are staring." He'd nudged her with his boot.

When she didn't respond, his eyes narrowed and his voice hardened. He leaned over her. "If you don't get up, I'll leave you here. It was just a stupid octopus. They'll get another one. Let's go."

Mylie had risen to her feet. To please Jake, she'd walked around and looked at the other creatures, but nothing warmed the cold void inside her. Soon after that day, Jake had started spending nights away from the house, and she rarely saw him anymore.

Now, turning away from the silence of Jake's bedroom, Mylie listened at the top of the stairs, her fingers gripping the banister. Her favorite jeans with the embroidered hearts brushed the tops of her sneakers. Her mother had stopped crying and Mylie could hear sounds of water running and cabinets opening. Shielded by darkness, she tiptoed down the steps. Her mother had hunched, grunting under her breath as she swept broken glass into a dustpan. Her body reminded Mylie of a marionette she used to play with whose floppy limbs had seemed loose in all the wrong places. She never liked the sound that the hard wood made when her legs and arms knocked together.

Mylie took the dustpan from her mother's hands and held it steady. They avoided each other's eyes. Mylie dropped glass shards into a trash bag and knotted it. She wiped down the counters while her mother filled the mop bucket. The mop made a wet splash on the floor as Mylie hefted the plastic bag over one shoulder.

The back door snapped shut behind her and she shivered in the wet air. Low fog curled around the trunks of the evergreens looming over the house. A swollen sun lit the trees in sickly green as it slid behind the mountains. Her tennis shoes squelched in the slick mud and she tread carefully to avoid falling. The front gate was open, and tire tracks gouged the damp soil where her father had spun out. Mylie tossed the trash in the bin and went to the back of the house, to the steep and overgrown trail that would take her to the beach. She grabbed tree roots and branches to steady herself and descended the slippery path.

Darkness fell as she reached the beach. Blurry yellow lights from houses on the far shore winked on like ghostly orbs. Slivers of pale moonlight peaked through purple clouds, illuminating a white buoy that bobbed in the middle of the canal. Silver-tipped waves rolled onto the shore. Mylie loved the endless dependability of the surf.

Wet sand clung to her sneakers as she wandered down the narrow beach. To the side of her, steep cliffs jutted into the sky. Foamy wave caps left seaweed in piles along the shore. The air was heavy with salt.

She wove her way through jagged rocks that dotted the sand like slumbering sea creatures. The tide ran in torrents around them. She found a dry spot and huddled against one of the rocks, facing cliffs that pressed out at her from the darkness with unspoken need. A deep cave gaped at the base of the cliffs. Jake had told her never to go into it. He said every couple of years someone disappeared fooling around in there, and no one ever found their bodies.

Mylie settled deeper and stretched her legs out in front of her. She scooped up sand and let it trickle through her fingers. As the light receded, twisted trees reached for the deepening sky, their branches swaying. It became difficult to see her hands. Two blue herons swooped overhead, huge wings gliding in eerie silence. They looked like the pterodactyls depicted in her dinosaur books, and she wondered if she had crossed into an alien world.

❧❧❧

"Mylie, wake up." Jake shook her. "Come on, you're gonna freeze out here."

She forced her eyes open. Her lips and nose were numb. Jake leaned over her, his heavy jacket zipped to his chin and a knit cap pulled to his brows. He rubbed her icy fingers, then took off his gloves and handed them to her.

"Put these on."

She obediently stuck her hands into the gloves, grateful for the warmth. He whipped off his jacket and wrapped it around her body, then sat next to her. The hard line of his shoulder pressed against hers, a solid weight.

"What did I tell you about coming out here like this? Remember that girl they found on the beach? You're gonna get yourself killed."

"Yeah, I remember." The collar of the jacket muffled Mylie's voice.

She followed Jake's gaze toward the yawning mouth at the bottom of the cliff. Gray fog had moved in over the canal, obscuring the lights of the houses. The cave was blacker than the silhouettes of the trees and seemed to breathe with a life of its own.

"I'm sorry." The thick mist swallowed her whisper.

"Come on, we gotta get back before Dad comes home." Jake switched on a flashlight and pulled Mylie to her feet.

That night Mylie dreamed she was swimming in a sea of endless green. Gleaming fish shimmied past her. Boneless, her body expanded and stretched as she slid effortlessly through hidden caves. She stretched out her tentacles, admiring her iridescent skin. They spread around her like a star as she let the tide carry her away.

❧❧❧

The smell of roasting chicken wafted through the house. Hot pads shrouded her mother's hands as she placed a steaming dish of vegetables on the table. A bowl of mashed potatoes, shiny with butter, already sat in the center. Mylie set the table and waited with Jake until their father sat down. Then they took their seats and unfolded napkins over their laps. Her mother was solicitous, quick to refill glasses and dole out second helpings. She barely ate anything herself. Even though conversation flowed around the table and forks clinked rhythmically on plates, the tension rose in the room like a bubble that will inevitably burst.

Once their father left the table and settled in front of the TV in the den, Jake jumped up and grabbed his coat. Mylie followed him.

"Are you going out?" She reached out and twisted her fingers in the hem of his sweater.

"Yeah." Jake tried to step away, the edge of his sweater entangled in Mylie's hand.

She took an awkward half step toward him. "Can I come too?"

Jake yanked her fingers from his sweater and turned away. "No, you can't. I'm not your babysitter."

He zipped his jacket and shoved his knit cap down on his head.

Her throat was tight and hot. Jake paused, put his hand on her shoulder. "We'll do something this weekend. I promise, okay?"

She nodded, still unable to speak. The front door closed behind him. In the den, her father's sharp voice cut through the drone of the TV as he said something to her mother.

The screaming began later. Mylie stared at a jumble of numbers on the pages of her math book as her father's angry voice pierced the floorboards and crashed into her bones. She slammed the book shut and curled up on her bed, hands clasped over ears.

More shouting, her mother pleading, and then a loud thwack. Unfamiliar rage boiled in Mylie and she sprinted down the stairs. Her mother had rolled into a tight ball on the floor, arms wrapped around her head. Welts sliced bright red against the white of her shoulders. The muscles in her father's jaw popped, his flat eyes reminding her of crushed pennies. He lifted his arm, ready to swing again.

The belt arced over the crouching body. Mylie wanted to go to her mother, but her legs wouldn't move. Her mouth filled with the hot, salty taste of blood when the belt found its mark on her mother. It whistled through the air again as she turned and ran, the back door slamming behind her.

She raced down the trail, branches tearing at her clothes. A gnarled root wound across the path and caught her foot. The world tumbled around her as she toppled and slid to the bottom of the trail. She lay dazed, her ankle throbbing.

After a while the drumming surf and the cool sand revived her. Spreading her hands, she scooped and let the grains slide between her fingers. She rolled on to her knees. The clouds had retreated, and Mylie stared up at the tapestry of stars in the onyx sky.

A brilliant streak flashed, followed by another. A meteor shower. Her pain momentarily forgotten, she watched the tongues of vivid white split the sky. As the flare of meteors slowed and blackness reclaimed the night, Mylie drifted.

The slither of something heavy scraping across rock woke her. She slunk down in the sand, holding her breath. The air was still, the contorted trees mute. Even the roar of the tide hushed in the face of overwhelming gloom. Mylie sensed life pulsing in the darkness, and she was afraid.

The thing moved again, this time behind her. Her eyes scanned the darkness beneath the cliffs. The mouth of the cave was no longer black, but glowed a brilliant green that cast an otherworldly luster on the surrounding rocks. The light dimmed as a shadow passed through the entrance. Mylie's heart pounded. She recognized the undulating movement.

The light beckoned, and she rose and limped across the sand to the cliff bottom. Piles of broken rock encircled the cave mouth. The light from the cave warmed her skin, reminding her of the soothing warmth she had felt when she was pressed against Ollie's aquarium.

She ducked to enter, hesitating just inside.

"Hello?"

Something slithered over the dry dirt of the cave. Mylie heard a wet sucking sound, then a voice reverberated inside her.

You smell of blood.

Mylie wrapped her arms around her chest. "I bit my lip."

You are frightened.

"He wouldn't stop hitting her. He never stops."

Silence. Mylie wiped a sudden tear from her eye.

"I don't ever want to go back to that place."

Come in. I will keep you safe.

Mylie moved deeper into the cave. A large shape rippled in the shadows.

Come closer.

Mylie stopped just at the edge of the darkness and settled cross-legged on the uneven ground.

"Is that you, Ollie? Did you come to take me away?"

Yes. If you follow me, you will never be afraid.

Inky tentacles glided out of the shadows. Raw pink tracks appeared on her skin where they touched, but she felt her fear and pain subsiding.

Following requires a sacrifice.

"I'll do anything to be with you, Ollie. Just tell me what I need to do."

A picture formed in Mylie's mind. "All?" she whispered.

They have all abandoned you.

The metallic tang of blood rose in her mouth like a promise.

❧❧❧

Mylie woke in the backyard, a tepid sun warming her face and grass stains on her jeans. Her ankle throbbed. She peeked around the front of the house. The car was gone so her father wasn't home. She entered through the back door and tiptoed upstairs. Her mother was in bed with the blinds tightly shut, her chest pumping up and down in quick raspy breaths.

The muted thump of bass shook the flimsy wood of Jake's closed door. She paused outside his room to knock but stopped with her fist raised in the air. Ollie had told her not to tell anyone of their meeting. The salty taste of blood lingered in her mouth and instead she went to her room. She stretched out on her bed and dreamed of floating in an endless ocean. When she woke, the sun was setting and beams of golden light dappled the walls. Her blanket tangled around her feet.

That evening she sat in the living room, eating Chinese food her father had brought home. He was in a generous mood and allowed them to watch TV while they ate, letting them pick the show. He had even surprised them with ice cream. She accepted her heaping bowl with a smile.

When the house was dark and silent, Mylie crept down the

stairs to the garage. Her father's can of lighter fluid sat on the shelf next to a stack of clean rags. She found the matches in a nearby drawer. She poured the fluid from the back door to the stairs, emptying the canister halfway up the risers. As she shook out the last few drops, chemical fumes stung her nose and eyes. She made her way back to the kitchen where a sudden image reared in her mind. Her mother curved over a bubbling pot on the stove, her back to Mylie, her shoulders a painted abstract of welts and bruises. Mylie's stomach clenched.

She twisted the knobs on the stove until she heard a sharp hiss from the burners. She waited at the back door as the pungent smell of gas filled her nostrils. The matches snapped like tiny twigs in her fingers several times before she managed to light one. The tiny flame caught hold, growing to a yellow flare that leapt and contorted, burning away the shadows of the house.

☙❧ ☙❧ ☙❧

Red and blue flashed on pine branches as a haze of smoke distorted the spinning lights of the emergency vehicles. To Mylie, hidden in the shadows, it looked like Christmas. Pieces of the shattered front door were strewn across the porch and entryway. Firemen in bright yellow jackets moved among the wreckage, their boots crunching over broken glass. Three stretchers stood in a neat row next to an ambulance. Blackened blood soaked through the white sheets.

Mylie slid into the darkness. Fog cloaked the trail, but her feet moved lightly, and she easily found her way to the glowing green light. She sat at the edge of the shadow, the scent of smoke and blood still smoldering inside her.

"Will you take me with you now?"

The wind played at the mouth of the cave, rustling clumps of serrated grass. The murky form shifted, and the rough walls of the cave faded. Mylie's thoughts dipped and spun like a pebble caught in the pull of a current. Her eyelids drooped. Beneath her lashes, silver waves rolled under a canopy of ancient stars. She let the warm buoyancy of the water take her. Unraveling, her body stretched and expanded, floating on a sea of green light. Her arms and legs split into a rippling eight-limbed star.

72

A tentacle snaked out of the shadows and lowered her body to the ground to wait for the inevitable rush of the tide.

THE WRAITH

by Kev Harrison

"Storm to starboard," came the call from the crow's nest. "Looks like a biggun'"

I scurried across the deck to the captain's quarters, almost crashing into the door as he bundled it open and stepped out into the fading daylight.

"I heard him, boy. Back to your post."

I nodded and backed away, not needing to be told twice. The Captain strode to the quarterdeck at the stern of the ship and snatched up the telescope from its chain next to the wheel.

"Someone's awoken old Davy, alright. Hard to port, men. Take in the main sails."

The small crew set to their tasks like clockwork. As Cabin Boy, my job was to do whatever anyone else told me to do. In this case it was to help the third mate haul in the main sails on the third mast. He heaved the great thick ropes down while I took hold of the slack, wrapping it around my arm and holding it fast. The *Siren*, a customized twelve cannon corvette, lurched as the rudder fought against the Caribbean currents to deliver us away from the tempest. A pirate vessel was not what my mother had envisaged, sending me out to learn the ropes at sea at the tender age of thirteen, after my father died. But these men were no monsters. We killed when we had to, but to a man this crew was far more interested in making their fortune than casting dead men adrift.

In a matter of minutes, we were sitting on the wet boards of the deck, brows soaked with sweat. The pilot had managed to alter our course. I looked out as great forks of lightning cracked the black sky and lit up the dark, unsettled sea. I stood and approached the gun rail to get a closer look. The captain, satisfied, returned to his quarters and all was quiet, but for the delayed echo of thunder every few moments. Then the *Siren* lurched to a halt, almost tossing me out into the black water. The door to the captain's quarters burst open and he was back out on deck, bellowing this time.

"There are rarely times in my life when I doubt my decisions, but at times like these, I wonder about asking for Mad Tom Fenn to come aboard as Bos'n. Where is that white-haired bastard?"

The question was not aimed at anyone in particular, and no one in particular was foolish enough to look at Captain Cocklyn in one of these moods, much less to address him. It wasn't necessary, anyway, as Mad Tom stepped down from behind the quarterdeck and onto the main deck.

"I had to drop the anchor Cap'n. Had no choice."

"You have sixty seconds to explain why, before I shoot you, as my Quartermaster has suggested so many times."

"This is where it happened, cap'n."

"Fifty-one."

"This, Cocklyn. This."

The bosun tugged at his thick white hair, jutting out of his head in all directions. All of twenty-six years old and said to have possessed a jet black shock of a barnet just two years earlier, everyone knew the story of how Mad Tom had gone white.

"The course we are on now, Cap'n. we're heading straight for Gun Cay."

The captain was not a great believer in fairy tales.

"And what of it, Fenn? It's a bloody island. We avoid the storm and then change course for Adeleide Village. We'll cash in this booty and be in our beds by lunch time. Better yet, a lady's bed."

"It's an island, Captain. That's the truth. But it's also the place where I saw the *Wraith*."

Two powder monkeys who should have been cleaning cannons overheard the words and let out an audible gasp. Captain Cocklyn eyed them harshly before he spoke.

"You will pull up the anchor, and we will be on our way in five minutes, or I'll find a bull shark that's a lot more real and a lot more dangerous than your imaginary *Wraith*. Do you understand me, Fenn?"

The bosun stroked his beard nervously, blinking.

"Aye sir."

He walked over to the stern and began winding the anchor winch. The *Siren* jerked forward as the squalls of the storm pushed into the sails and we were off once more.

⚒⚒⚒

It wasn't long before midnight that I came back on to the deck from my duties in the kitchen. There was little more than a skeleton crew on deck at this time, the second mate taking his turn at the wheel. One of the gunners stayed out, ready to help with the rigging. Everyone else was trying to catch some sleep. All except Mad Tom. I went over to have a word. As I got closer, I could see his skin almost glow against the dark of the night. It was so pale it matched the snowy tone of his hair, brows and beard. I sat beside him.

"You don't look well, Tom."

"Wait, Jacob. Just wait, and keep your eyes fixed beyond the prow."

I looked over and saw a bright point in the distance ahead.

"I don't think we'll wait much longer, Fenn. Look."

Mad Tom was on his feet and rushing to the bow of the ship, leaning out into the gloom of the night. He turned back to me, the whites of his eyes great saucers against the sky.

"I'll not get away this time. None of us will."

He turned and bolted towards the stern and disappeared into the captain's quarters.

⚒⚒⚒

I can't tell you how many minutes I sat there on the barrel of that forward cannon, watching as the hypnotic glow of flame rippled like liquid from miles away. It couldn't be any bigger than a schooner, by the look of it. The way it burned, no one could possibly have survived.

"They was pirates, just like us, lad."

The gunner had walked up the deck to take a look. He clutched a portable telescope in his hand. He passed it to me.

"They're flying old Captain Death, just like us."

I held the scope up to my eye, adjusted the focusing lens. Every inch of the boat was aflame. The sails, too, were florid with fierce gold and orange, though they somehow still strained with the force of the wind. And the flag. The Jolly Roger. Still it billowed,

77

somehow escaping the inferno.

"Benito," I handed the telescope back. "This must be the first Jolly Roger I've seen with horns protruding from the skull."

The Spaniard's expression turned hollow, desperate.

"What did you say?"

I went to repeat myself, but he held his palm in front of me, instead raising the eyeglass once more.

"*Cristo me salve.*"

He dropped the eye glass and sprinted astern, to the bridge. He waved his muscular arms to the second mate.

"Turn the ship around. You *have to* turn around. It's the *Wraith*!"

The second mate looked aghast, his eyes darting from his despairing crewmate to the shimmering speck of flame edging closer with every breath of the cool wind. I held my position at the bow, not knowing what to do.

The captain's door finally swung open, Cocklyn striding out on to the deck. The gunner threw himself to his knees in front of him and pleaded with the captain to change course.

"Your delusions are contagious, Fenn."

He spat the words in the direction of the bosun, who now clutched a bottle of rum from the raid in Havana in his trembling right hand. Cocklyn approached the wheel and held up the telescope, fixing his gaze on the ship. He began to chuckle. The chuckle grew, spreading into his barrel chest, becoming a haughty laugh as he once again lowered the eyeglass to behold his crew.

"A half-singed schooner, adrift in the night and suddenly my brave pirate men are cowering and crying ghost ship. Boy!" He was calling to me. "Go and wake the men, preferably the non-cowards, and tell them to prepare the cannon!"

I took one last look at the blazing vessel and scuttled off below deck.

⚓⚓⚓

It can't have been more than a few minutes before I was back on deck, flanking every one of the powder monkeys and gunners we had on board. They took their positions, dragging barrels of gunpowder and bags of shot. The second mate, still acting pilot, used only the gaff sails to manoeuvre the *Siren* into firing position. At my tender age, I still had no real understanding of the dangers of piracy, so the process of readying the *Siren* for battle was one of excitement for me. That naivety was to die the moment I turned to port, laying eyes for the first time on our quarry from close in.

It was still a little over a hundred feet from shooting distance, but this was clearly no ordinary ship. Every plank that made up the schooner was coated with liquid flame, flickering and rushing over it as it silently encroached on us. Fire danced on the sails and the ropes. Tongues of burning red licked at the fabric, but left no scorch marks. No smoke rose from the vessel. Perhaps most sinister of all, the ship's captain, wearing a simple tricornered hat and peasant's clothes, glared at us from the middle of the deck, fire washing over him, illuminating his narrow face and sunken eyes.

The quartermaster, now organising the gunners, bellowed his commands. I swallowed hard as I watched the powder monkeys clean the barrels of the eight portside cannons before the gunners tilted their weapons up and sent out a volley. The first two cannonballs to break water were wayward, but the next four were right on target, but they seemed to pass straight through the vessel. The quartermaster looked up to the bridge, eyes pleading with Captain Cocklyn for what to do next.

"Fire again, man. Fire again!"

Cocklyn still refused to be swayed by superstition. The gunners set to work.

I looked around me for Fenn. What could he tell us about his *Wraith*, if indeed that was the ship we were facing. I left my station at the hatch and ran inside. Mad Tom had curled into a ball in the corner of the gunners' quarters. It was no more than a line of cots and smelt of rancid sweat, owing to the cramped conditions.

"Mad Tom! You wouldn't believe what I've just seen up there."

Mad Tom's eyes were open. Unblinking. But also unfocussed. I waved my hand in front of his face.

"I hear you, boy. But what to tell you? Is it comfort you seek? You'll take none from me."

"I'll take comfort from understanding what in hell's going on up there, sir."

"Understanding is something you'll never manage. But let me

show you this."

Fenn lifted his shirt to reveal a ruined, contorted panel of skin along his lateral muscles, criss-crossed with the knitted signature of burn scars. I raised my hand to my mouth to hide my disgust.

"That was from the first time I saw the *Wraith*, boy. It wasn't so long ago. Just two years. We tried the cannon just the same. His majesty's royal naval cannon at that. Threw everything we had at her. But she kept coming. Her captain's eyes fixing us all where we remained until the flames engulfed everything. I stood, smelling our flesh cook, but I couldn't move. Not until Henry fired his musket. That's when I ran, jumped overboard, fire still eating me as I doused myself in the frigid sea. The next thing I know I washed up, knotted in the sea weed on Williams island, with a new hair-do."

He tugged at his white locks. I tried to look into his eyes, but the madness there – the despair – forced me to look away.

"And this time?"

The question drifted in the squalid air.

"No such hopes this time, boy."

I told him that I had to return to the deck, that I might be needed. He nodded and pulled his knees into his body, adopting a foetal position once more. Just as I opened the door, he called after me.

"Boy. Don't listen to the voice."

"What voice?"

"You'll know."

I ran out of the room to the steps and up on to the deck.

The sea was eerily calm and bathed in near daylight. The burning ship had moved ever closer while I'd been below with Mad Tom. I could make out the features of the captain. His pale skin highlighted his gaunt face, his eyes sunken so deeply that the thick rings of purple and black only accentuated the reflections of the flames dancing across them.

I looked about me, the men on my ship clearly shaken as a third volley of shot was being prepared in the six portside cannons. The gunners' expressions spoke more of hope than belief as they lined up the barrels. Ignited. Fired. Watched as the ship simply kept coming. Six misses from point blank range. I had seen these men work these last fifteen months. They were crack shots. They didn't miss.

The quartermaster took off his hat and looked with pleading eyes to the captain, still watching on from his vantage point on the bridge. Cocklyn surveyed the scene before him, tugging at his long beard. Finally he gave the order.

"Turn her around, men. Drop the sails, once we're straight. Evasive measures, all hands!"

The acting pilot immediately rolled the wheel hard to his right, to turn us to starboard and towards the forested west coast of Paradise Island. The quartermaster began to bark commands to the gunners, to abandon their stations and prepare to work the rigging. Then he stopped mid-sentence. He turned to face the oncoming ship and his face went pale. He looked directly across to the captain of the other ship. He stood for a moment, looking forward. A gentle nod. Another. He whispered something unintelligible. Then he closed his eyes, drew his musket from his belt and held it to his head, firing the round into his brain before the nearest gunner could stop him. He slumped to the deck, blood pooling around him.

I was still gawking at the crimson liquid seeping from his ruined brain when I heard my name.

"Jacob."

A whisper. The voice spoke again, this time slightly louder, gentle, as if into my ear from up close. I spun around.

"Mother?"

The third mate looked at me, cocking his head and offering me a quizzical expression.

"I ain't your mother, lad."

I felt myself flush.

"No. No. I'm sorry."

I heard her again.

"Jacob. Listen to me."

My eyes darted one way and then the other. She was nowhere to be seen. I had to be imagining it. The trauma, perhaps.

"Jacob. When you went away to sea, I never thought you'd be a filthy pirate."

My heart started to thump faster in my chest.

"You've brought great shame to your family, son."

She was so close, but nowhere to be seen.

"Take that knife, Jacob. Take the knife from your belt."

I pulled my knife from its sheath with my right hand and lifted it in front of my face.

"Now turn it to that wretched neck of yours and cut deep, boy."

I froze, the knife still held out in front of me. Mad Tom's warning. The voice. I looked across to the other ship, watched as the captain spoke with my mother's voice. His eyes boring into my flesh and draining my will power with every passing moment. I cast my knife to the ground and watched it slide along the deck until it was out of sight. My mother's voice disappeared immediately. His eyes left mine and darted to the next in line.

I watched as the nearest powder monkey lifted his barrel and began to drink down a trail of course gunpowder. He spluttered as he swallowed the dark powder, dropping the barrel on to the deck and walking out to one of the rowboats. I knew what was coming, but my legs refused me permission to intervene. He lowered the boat down into the unnaturally flat sea, pushed off from the *Siren* and lit his flint. Splintered ends of wood were all that was left visible on the surface of the water. The smell of cooked flesh and burnt hair blended with the salty air.

As the smoke from the explosion cleared, my attention returned to the burning ship, close enough now to feel the heat emanating from it. Despite the lack of wind or wave, the flag atop the single mast billowed furiously, seemingly bringing the horned skull to life, its eyes intricately-painted pools of fire. My eyes darted to its captain, his features drawn tightly across his skull. His eyes, too, seemed to be alive with fire. More than just a reflection of the inferno surrounding him. He burned from within.

"What can we do, Captain?"

I implored Cocklyn, still silently staring, open mouthed at the fallen quartermaster. He looked at me, his eyes totally empty of ideas. Of strength. Of will.

Then, impact.

The hull shook violently as the ironclad ram of the Wraith made first contact with the *Siren*, splintering the walls of one of the bunk rooms below. Seemingly from nowhere, a mass of men began to swarm across to our deck on ropes and boards. Each of them bore the same pale, gaunt appearance of near death. Each of them with features illuminated by a fire that needed neither fuel nor air to burn.

I looked about me. Watched as pilot, gunners, and every soul around me was taken without weapons, the crew of the Wraith doing naught more than reach out and touch my crewmates, sending them collapsing to the ground, unconscious. Perhaps dead. It was instant. I watched and stood and did nothing. *Could* do nothing to help my crewmates. I spun again and again, watching them fall, one after another.

Then I stopped perfectly still. My breath left me. The Wraith's captain stood before me. Eyes of fire bore into mine. I felt a frigid wave of ice spread through my body from my heart. Paralysed, I tried to speak. To breathe. Managed neither. Then he reached forward with his hand. Pressed it to my bare arm. Gripped it.

I watched as my skin began to glow, pull tighter over my flesh and then I felt the burning. My entire body ablaze. I stepped back, looked once more into those burning eyes. He smiled.

I don't know how long it had been since that moment when I awoke. Whether "awoke" is the right word, I'm still not sure.

'Man your station, boy.'

I heard it, but the man sitting on my bunk hadn't spoken. I sat up, looked at my skin. The burns, the scarring were gone. My flesh was tight over my bones, skin a milky white. I stood and followed the wooden steps on to the deck and into a roaring blaze.

The captain turned, those burning eyes once again boring into mine.

'A new quarry awaits the *Wraith*, lad.'

He, too, spoke without sound. I nodded and looked over his shoulder. A crescent moon hung low over the sea, casting the faintest of lights over a merchant vessel. I heard a bell ringing from the deck of the ship, saw crew members rushing one way and the other. Then I felt the flames in my eyes roar and dance with hunger.

KELPIE 5

by K. Lawrence

The rigs rose out of the rain and mist like great alien ships. Their towers tore at the sky. Their legs stood defiantly in the tumultuous waves of the North Sea, never moving yet always under strain, constantly at war with the elements they called home. Kelpie 5, a maze of a structure in the usual red and gray, with a great flame bursting from the top of its tower like a signal beacon, slowly came into view. It was dwarfed by its larger cousins, Gorilla 2 and the enormous Colloden Alpha, which was large enough to be seen from the upper deck of the Kelpie. Cameron Stewart, a newly hired roustabout, couldn't take his eyes from it. The tiny rig was going to be his home for the next two weeks.

The helicopter swayed in the strong winds as it wound lazily towards the platform. For a hair raising moment they swung wide of the helipad. The steel gray sea surged up the supports towards them as the pilots fought to bring the helicopter down. Finally, the wheels hit the platform and the men filed out into the wind and rain. Cameron lurched sideways under the force of the gusts.

So, this was Kelpie 5? Renowned black gold mine, a tiny powerhouse of a rig which workers fought to be on. Because of the amount of oil it spewed out, the pay on Kelpie was generous— Cameron would bring home three thousand pounds more than he would on any other platform.

The ground shook under his feet. The steel legs groaned, or perhaps Cameron imagined they did. The waves certainly looked like they were slamming into them enough to cause the metal to squeal. Rain lashed down, soaking them through in the few seconds it took to cross the deck. They clumped through claustrophobic hallways until they were deposited into a large canteen. Cameron swayed slightly and his ears rang in the relative silence. No one else seemed affected, so he wrote it off as simply not having acclimatized yet.

A couple of workers wearing kitchen whites walked among them with trays of steaming mugs. Cameron gratefully took one. The heat felt good in his hands. It tasted slightly sour, especially for a drink that looked like thick hot chocolate, perhaps it was a special recipe? When he asked the kitchen staff all he got was a smile, then the cook tapped the side of his nose with his finger, indicating it was a secret. Cameron shrugged. The drink probably had some sort of alcohol in it to chase the chill out of the new recruits. He downed the rest without much thought.

The seasoned workers headed off quickly to their assigned quarters while Cameron and a small group of new starts remained in the canteen. A rich, meaty scent, probably some sort of stew with a thick gravy, wafted out from behind the shining steel counters, and despite the howling weather outside and his wet clothes, Cameron felt a little warmer. His belly rumbled as the scent continued to creep up his nostrils. His hope that the stew would be passed out among them just like the strange chocolate drink was quickly dashed when a woman stepped into the room and introduced herself as Mary, the head of health and safety. Soon the new workers were being led around the rig like obedient dogs. Living quarters here, equipment rooms there. Medical on the second floor. HR and admin on the third. Safety clothing must be worn on the top deck. And never, ever, venture down onto the lower floors alone. Cameron's gaze drifted towards the red handrails that marked the way down to the seemingly forbidden lower level.

"Why can't I go down there?" he asked.

Mary huffed air through her nose. "Not just you, anyone. This is an old platform, and some of it is in bad need of repairs." She made a casual gesture towards the stairs. "The lowest level isn't used for anything nowadays except housing for the rats and crap that has no place anywhere else. If you ever have a need to go down there, which is a rarer occurrence than a blue moon, you'll be sent in pairs."

Cameron shuddered. The mere thought of a forbidden floor, no doubt cluttered with rusting pipework and arthritic machinery, made his skin crawl. What slimy, wriggling creatures, or perhaps even scuttering, furry ones, had chosen to call the abandoned floor home? He was all too happy when they returned to the living quarters.

His room was much better than Cameron had expected. It was a bit on the small side, but clean, and in perfect condition. He threw his bag onto the top bunk, claiming it before his roommate could.

"Oh, so that's how it is?" said an amused voice from the vicinity of the doorway. "You know, seniority is power here. I should get first choice of bunk." The owner of the voice was a short man with arms like coiled rope and long, straggly blond hair. He held out his hand. "Ben Foster."

Cameron shook Ben's hand. "Cameron Stewart."

"First timer?" Ben inquired as he tossed his own bag onto the lower bunk. Cameron confirmed with a nod. "Don't worry, we'll keep you right. It's a tight knit group of guys here."

"Thanks," Cameron replied. "Looks like it's a good place to work."

Ben busied himself with unpacking and making his bunk space more homely. "It has it's good and bad points." He glanced at Cameron, and for a second something darker lurked behind Ben's sunny disposition. "Just keep your head down, don't draw too much attention to yourself, and you'll be fine."

Cameron frowned. "Well, okay. I'll try."

Ben's warm smile returned. "Great! Our first shift starts in a few hours. Do you want to grab something to eat before then?"

Cameron agreed. It was time to scope out the other occupants of the rig.

⚜ ⚜ ⚜

The canteen was busy when they arrived. Ben talked incessantly, explaining how the meals worked and where to get everything. Once they had been served, he steered the way through the tables and sat at one already occupied by three other guys.

"Lads, this is Cameron. He's a new start," Ben said by way of an introduction.

The other men grunted their hellos then returned to their food. Cameron followed their lead and didn't bother carrying on the conversation. A few words were exchanged here and there between the men who knew one another, but nothing more exciting than a "pass the salt," or "are you sitting on my newspaper?" Cameron looked around the other tables. The mostly male night-shift crew had maybe thirty workers in total of all different ages. No one really seemed to be talking to anyone else.

Somewhere deep inside the rig, metal screeched as it strained.

Someone was watching him.

Across the canteen sat a man who didn't look away like the others had. He was older, though his long grey hair seemed at odds with his strongly muscled body and angular face. His bulging arms were covered in bio-organic tattoos—seething masses of tentacles constructed from stone, bone, and swirls that brought to mind the inside of snails' shells. The man's eyes were the same steel grey as the sea that threatened to sweep Kelpie away, and as they stared at one another, the irises seemed to darken.

"Have you made a friend?" Ben smirked.

Cameron averted his eyes and smarted as Ben and the others laughed. "He was staring at me first."

The sensation of being watched remained. When he eventually looked up the man was still looking at him, a ghost of a smile playing over his thin lips.

❦ ❦ ❦

The same heavy clouds that had hung low over the rig when Cameron had first arrived became an impenetrable blanket by night. Down on the platform, he and the other roustabouts worked under the harsh glow of artificial lights, manning the immense pumps that kept the drill holes clear. A tear in the line had soaked them all through within minutes of starting their shift, but they soldiered on, fighting wind, rain, sea, even their own bodies that wanted nothing more than rest and warmth. Through his ear defenders Cameron could still pick up the roar of the equipment and the howling of the skin-peeling wind. In the brief silences the rig creaked and whined under the assault from its hostile environment and uttered groans as if it were a giant sighing in complaint. More than once, Cameron spotted his fellow roustabouts patting the rig on the closest available surface, as if comforting some titanic creature. He was unable to ask anyone why—the wind stole his voice whenever he tried—but by break time he was finding the behaviour endearing and even patted Kelpie himself. The wall felt slimy under his gloves, an effect of the rain and oil that was ever present.

88

Cameron could have wept for joy when he followed the others back inside to spend the coffee break in the warm confines of the canteen. He lagged behind the others, his leaden legs refusing to cooperate. Would he last his first two weeks out here? Possibly not if the weather didn't let up.

A deep, heaving sigh echoed through the hallways, a strange mix of a dog's yawn and the usual groans of the rig at work. He doubled back to stare down the other adjoining walkway, which lay completely empty.

The fine hairs along the back of his neck shivered.

There was nothing there. He told himself again and again. There were no shadows for a thing to hide in. No doorways for someone to have run into. It was just one long, well-lit hallway.

No! Something was down there. It was just out of sight, but Cameron knew it was there, and it knew that he knew it was there. Cameron held his breath. His stomach fluttered with a sudden attack of nerves, and still nothing happened.

He moved on reluctantly when Ben shouted his name.

✿✿✿

The next day, as Cameron sleepily ambled from his room to the canteen, he heard it again. The rest of the workers carried on walking, no one paying attention to the rumble that Cameron could feel as well as hear, but they were seasoned rig hands. Perhaps the rumble was the generators or similar machinery that kept the rig alive.

A whine, halfway between a metallic squeal and a human wail, rushed through the hallway on icy breath. He fought every instinct and moved toward the noise.

It led him downstairs.

Every time he came close to considering turning back he heard it again. It was almost mournful yet with a tinge of rage.

Cameron hesitated at the top or the last set of steps, held in place by the same force that kept children in their time-out spots. Curiosity soon overpowered it. He placed his foot onto the first step. When the rig didn't collapse around him, he took another step, and then another, until he hit the landing that formed the midway point of the staircase. Below him, the last floor was poorly lit, and water dripped ceaselessly. A cold wind rushed upstairs, wrapped him up in its icy blanket, then moved on. It carried another metallic sigh with it. Gingerly, Cameron made his way down to the hallway. Patches of rust blighted the walls, the ceiling, the floor, and slick puddles gleamed in between. How was this safe? The integrity of the rest of the rig would suffer surely.

Cameron leaned out to look down the hallway, not quite brave enough to step onto forbidden ground, then rested his hand on a pipe to steady himself as he finally left the stairs.

The pipe moved.

Cameron jerked his hand back and clutched it to his chest. The pipe peeled itself from the wall and slithered down the hallway, moving faster and faster through the stagnant puddles until it disappeared around a bend. He stood frozen in place, fear and disbelief warring for dominance. Down the hallway, a churning, squelching sound that brought to mind maggots in a bucket echoed. The lights flickered.

Something moved, writhing and wrapping itself around the metal walls and exposed piping. They edged closer, a slimy, seething mass of eels filling the entire hallway.

He screamed and tried to run.

The metal under him gave way like wet cardboard. Cameron landed hard on his knees. Behind him, the slugs surged closer, their oil-slick bodies sucking and squelching against the rusting metal. He hauled his foot out of the hole, leaving a good portion of skin behind, and bolted up the stairs. He kept running until he reached the canteen.

"Come with me right now!" his words tumbled out in a garbled rush.

His roommate narrowed his eyes. "Why? What's up with you?"

"Just come with me now! Please!" He glanced at the others at the table, who were regarding him with amused expressions. "I need you to see this."

Finally, Ben got up. They headed through the rig together, Ben grumbling about being taken away from his breakfast, the wasted journey, everything he could think of.

"You'll get us fired," Ben said in one last complaint.

"Then turn back," Cameron answered sharply. "But, believe

me, you'll want to see this." Or maybe it was more that he just wanted someone to tell him he wasn't crazy.

Ben grumbled under his breath but followed Cameron regardless. Both of them hesitated at the top of the steps, but a look and an unspoken agreement sent them both downwards into the well-lit hallway. There was no rust, no puddles, nothing. Had he taken the wrong stairs? Was it just one area that was rusted?

"Why aren't we allowed down here?" he asked in the vain hope Ben's answer would clear up the mystery.

Ben shrugged. "There are plenty of no-go places. It's not our job to as—" he fell into silence at the sound of voices above them. They ran as silently as they could manage in work boots into the first room in the hallway. The voices faded away without ever reaching their hiding place.

"Is this what you wanted to show me?" Ben grumbled and gestured towards an old generator lurking against the far wall. "It's an old rig. There's a ton of this stuff."

"No. There's a section down here that's all rusted and decaying," Cameron insisted.

"Then let's go find it," Ben suggested. "We're in a forbidden area already; might as well make the most of it."

Cameron was too happy at the prospect of leaving the room and its elderly occupant behind to question Ben's sudden change of heart. Together, they walked the entirety last floor. They found plenty of old machinery, a few rooms filled with junk, a few more tiny patches of water damage, but no sign of a rotted hallway. The last room finally offered up something weird.

"What the hell is this?" Cameron whispered as he stepped inside. On every available surface sat pillar candles. In one corner rested a pile of thick blankets and a few pillows. Unidentifiable dark spots painted the walls, ceiling, and floor.

"We are stuck out here for two weeks. Can't get home, can't do the usual stuff we would. Maybe this is where some of the workers get together and work out their... frustrations," Ben said with a smirk.

Cameron rolled his eyes. "It's not like we're stuck here for years."

"No, but some people have weird ideas about entertainment." He patted Cameron's shoulder. "Let's go. There's nothing down here but some love nest."

"But I saw it!" Cameron insisted. "The floor was rusted. There was these huge slug things. I hurt my leg when the floor gave way." He pulled up his trouser leg but all there was only a large bruise, not the skinned shin he had expected. He let the material drop. "I've been hearing all sorts of weird shit too."

"You're just having a hard time adjusting. Who doesn't get bruises in this job?" Ben nodded his head toward the door. "We should get back up before someone finds us."

Reluctantly, Cameron followed Ben from the room, but he couldn't resist one last look down the hallway. For a second, he thought he saw creeping, slug-like tentacles, but it was just the lights and the curve of the hallway playing tricks.

☠☠☠

The wind and rain had ceased. Even the waves no longer threw themselves at the rig with suicidal abandon. Cameron shivered, and not because of the ever present cold. The world appeared to be holding its breath, watching, waiting but for what? He had no clue except for the ever present roiling, unassigned anxiety in stomach.

At least it felt safer for working so close to the edge of the platform. Cameron knelt inches away from the sheer drop, repairing part of the deck that had come loose. He looked down towards the unusually calm waves and saw a small, shadowy shape hurtle down into the surf. The waves parted and a huge beak, dragging seaweed and foaming seawater, opened wide. It snapped shut over the shadow and disappeared below the sea once more. Dark tentacles, almost as thick as the rig's legs, whipped towards him. Cameron scrambled back from the edge and dropped his rivet hammer. It clanged heavily on the deck.

Cameron scrambled to his feet, picked up his hammer, and got back to work without a word. What was the point in saying anything? No one would believe him and, as the world moved on unchanged by what he saw, he began to doubt his own recollection too. Every so often he peeked over the edge, just to see if he could spot the beak in the waves again. The sea remained calm, undisturbed.

"A sensible man would not be hanging off the side like that," said a gruff voice behind him.

Cameron spun around and came face to face with the tattooed man. "I was just... I was watching what I was doing," Cameron muttered. He wanted to turn away, but something in the man's gaze held him in place.

"I've been watching you, Cameron," he said, his voice barely rising above a whisper. "And if I see you then *it* sees you." His grin was wolfish, disarming. Cameron fought the urge to back away.

Without another word, the tattooed man walked away. Cameron half expected him to disappear, to be some strange apparition, but he stayed reassuringly solid until he stepped below deck.

"Did you see that?" he asked Danny, who was working closest to him. When he got no response he gave Danny's shoulder a little shove.

Danny removed his ear defenders. "What?"

"That guy with all the tattoos was up in my face just then. Did you see him?"

"Sam?" Danny shook his head. He's a janitor, he doesn't work up top."

"But I just saw..."

"Can't have," Danny stated, cutting him off. "He doesn't work up top."

Cameron tutted loudly and gave up his questioning. It was possible Danny simply didn't see Sam, since he had been bent over his work. Regardless, all this dismissal of what he was hearing and seeing was making him doubt his own sanity. From now on, he was breaking the rules and taking his phone everywhere. The next time something happened, he was recording it.

※ ※ ※

Cameron's sleep was dreamless, and for the first time in five days he woke up feeling refreshed. He was in a good mood until he entered the canteen. The atmosphere was heavy, dark.

"What's wrong with everyone?" he quietly asked as he sat at his usual table.

"Mick died last night," Eric muttered without looking up from his porridge.

"How?"

There were shrugs all around.

"It's a rig; it's dangerous. And that means people die," added Danny.

"How do they know he died if no one knows what happened?" Cameron asked. Again, there were shrugs all around. He considered telling them about what he saw, but figured it would get him nothing but more rolled eyes and condescending looks. They were right anyway. Death and injury was an unfortunate part of the job. Even with all the safeguards in place, they couldn't control nature. All it took was a lightning storm or a badly timed gust of wind and it was lights out.

He went back to eating and tried to put everything out of his mind, but the thoughts rose their ugly heads again and again. He looked over at Sam, who stared back with a small smile on his lips. The puzzle pieces slowly clicked together.

His spoon stood upright for a second in his porridge before it keeled over. He pushed the food away in disgust and got up from the table.

Ben was on Cameron's heels as he left the cafeteria. "What's wrong with you?"

"There's something really weird going on here," Cameron said in a conspiratorial whisper. "All those things I keep seeing and hearing. Someone dying and no one knowing how? What are you hiding?"

Ben's face darkened with anger. "No one is hiding anything. It's an oil rig. Unfortunately, people die. It's a dangerous job, and no one is watched twenty-four hours a day. So, yeah, sometimes people die and no one knows what happened for sure."

Cameron looked around. The hallways were empty. "I saw him," he admitted.

"Saw who?"

Without really planning it, the whole story came tumbling out of him. Ben listened and occasionally shook his head.

"I think he's poisoning me, making me hallucinate." Cameron said in a conspiratorial whisper. "Maybe he did the same to the lad who died before he threw him off the rig."

Ben laughed. "You have a good imagination, Cameron. Maybe you can make a career out of writing stories once they throw you off the rig for being batshit crazy."

"I am not batshit!" Cameron snapped. "I know what I saw!"

"But it wasn't there when I went with you, remember?"

Cameron sighed wearily. "It wasn't there because someone is spiking my food."

"You know what?" Ben hissed. "If you really believe that then go tell the bosses or the police."

"Maybe I will!" he retorted and stormed angrily away.

By the time he reached the health and safety office, Cameron had decided against giving the full story. Instead he kept his tale to the weird noises and unsettling images. Mary seemed unconcerned.

"It's a strange environment with a lot of stress," she said in an annoyingly patronising tone. "I can assure you that there is nothing strange going on in this rig. It's the same as any other in the North Sea."

"But all this stuff I keep—"

"Has anyone else seen anything, heard anything?" she asked, cutting him off.

Cameron shook his head. "No, but they wouldn't if—"

"No one is poisoning the food," she said as if speaking to someone without all their mental faculties. "Do you really believe someone would target you alone?"

"No," Cameron finally conceded. "It just seemed to be the most plausible explanation."

Mary clasped her hands under her chin like a priest or headteacher and leaned forward a little in her chair. "I understand that the first few weeks working on a rig are a huge adjustment, especially for someone starting on night-shift So, I want you to put all this out of your mind until you go home at end of next week. If you still feel this way after the break then don't come back." She flicked through a pile of papers on her desk. "We don't really expect everyone who thinks they are able to work out here to actually last."

Cameron bit down hard on his angry retort. "I can do this job."

"Then prove it."

They stared at each other until Cameron looked away. Without another word he left her office and headed up to the top deck to work. He'd show them all. The first sound, the first creepy thing he saw, and he was going to record it. Where would their condescending looks be then?

❀❀❀

Maybe it *had* all been in his head?

The last days of his first stint passed without incident. No strange groans in the hallways. No pipes that recoiled at his touch. Even Sam seemed to have dropped his staring. Free to concentrate on his job, Cameron began to enjoy his work and the company he was in. Determined to prove himself to his boss after all he had said, Cameron worked hard and took any new task that came up. It was almost a shame to be leaving, even if he and the others from his work shift would be back in three weeks.

On the last morning, Cameron's eyes were open before the rest of him realised he was awake. Ben slept on, snoring softly. Elsewhere, the day shift was hard at work. Cameron closed his eyes, unsure of what had woken him, and tried to grab a few more seconds sleep.

This time, he heard it.

It was like a long, drawn out intake of breath mixed with the rumbling of an elephant. It sounded as if it came from big lungs, from huge vocal chords, and it sounded content. It was too familiar a noise for Cameron to let it slide. He *had* to investigate.

He dropped silently to the floor and pulled a spare boiler suit over the top of his pyjamas. He waited until he was in the hallway before putting his boots on. As much as he would like company, he knew what Ben's reaction would be, what all their reactions had been. Complete scepticism and annoyance.

The grumble reached his ears again. Cameron followed it down through the levels of the rig, nodding to the day shift as if he was just another guy going about his work, and finally reached the steps to the lowest level. The sound was definitely coming from down there. He was so close to whatever was making it that it rattled his ribs like a powerful bassline. He crept down the steps and was relieved to find the hallway as clean and bright as when he and Ben checked it. Still, the memory of the slithering pipe kept him from touching the walls. Cameron edged his way down the hallway. Each step was placed with the utmost care, minimising noise and testing for any weak parts in the floor. The door to the middle room on the left-hand side stood ajar. The purring came from inside. Cameron crept up to the door and peeked inside.

Large pillar candles sat around the edges of the room, painting it in flickering yellows and blacks. The floor, the walls, even the ceiling, were spattered with dark marks, and in the centre of it all knelt Sam, stroking a huge granite-coloured tentacle as if it was a very large cat. As Cameron's eyes adjusted to the poor light, he saw more of the same stone-like tentacles rising up through the hole in the floor and clinging to the wall like huge slugs. They all rippled as one. The purr was almost deafening this time.

Sam made a noise in return, similar to the rumble from the beast. It was almost like throat singing. The creature answered with a more musical, intoned version of the grumbles and breaths Cameron had heard before.

Cameron couldn't move. His body was reacting to the sight with shaking knees and a nauseating pain in his stomach, but his brain refused to process it. He stood there and stared.

The door creaked loudly with an accidental nudge from his foot.

The tentacles reared up and shook like the tails of rattlesnakes. Sam whipped around, his eyes like black holes in his face. He had taken two strides forward before Cameron had the presence of mind to run.

Outside, the hallway melted away to reveal an aged, rusted version of itself. The pipework warped and turned to spit at him. The floor rocked and bucked under his feet. He made it to the stairwell and took them two at a time, refusing to look back until he reached his room.

Cameron grabbed Ben by the shoulders and shook him out of sleep.

"It's after me!" he shouted before Ben could chastise him for the rude awakening.

Ben smiled sadly. "You could have left," he whispered. "One more day and you would have been free." Ben gripped his wrists painfully and got out of bed. He dragged Cameron back into the hallway.

"I told you several times," he said with a shake of his head. "It's different out here; life takes a bit of adjustment." The ceiling above their heads turned to a rotting mess. Gnarled pipes lay strewn across the floor. "Well, this rig," Ben continued, "takes more adjustment than most."

A large section of door lintel bent outwards from the wall with a sharp creek. It's razor point sloped downwards, reaching for their flesh. Cameron jerked out of the way.

"Help! You have to help me!" Cameron shouted at a worker who stepped into the hallway. The woman looked at them both with hollow eyes. The flesh slowly peeled from her bones and she crumbled to the floor. Cameron screamed.

"Hush. It won't make any difference," Ben said. He stepped nimbly over a hole that had appeared in the floor. "We can't deny each other's existence any longer."

"What the hell are you talking about?"

Ben continued to walk without answering. His flesh slowly disintegrated and absorbed into the floor. Cameron ripped his arm out of Ben's bony grasp, threw his unwilling legs into a run, and fled for the top deck.

The rig crumbled around him as he ran. Some of his fellow riggers fled with him while others melted into the rusting hulk. He leapt for the top deck, but his foot never touched the step. The staircase rose up to meet him, and he landed hard. Not a breath remained in his body.

The whole journey replayed in reverse as he was dragged back through the rig. He slammed against walls, smashed his arm on the side of the door, but moved ever onwards. The structure shook with the bellow of the creature that held him firm.

A roustabout screamed as he fell through a gaping crack at the bottom of a stair case. Putrid orange liquid dripped from the rusting surfaces all around them. Kelpie 5 was a wreck! A rotted, skeletal structure held together by Verdigris and sheer force of will. The farther down he went, the more decomposed it became. Tentacles crowded any available surface. They wrapped around him, the stone hide ripping his exposed skin and threatening to tear his boiler suit.

Cameron landed heavily on a metal floor. Candles flickered all around. He rolled onto his back and tried to breathe, but his lungs seemed to contain shattered glass.

"Look at you, perfectly tenderised," Sam laughed. "You will make a good meal."

Cameron tried to speak, but his mouth was full of broken teeth. Sam knelt by his side. One of the tentacles settled around his neck and snuggled against his cheek.

"I knew you could see through the illusion," Sam said in a soft voice. "I suppose it had to happen again eventually. I was the same when I first started here." He petted the tentacle lovingly. "This rig is nothing but a rotting shell, but you knew that, right? And our friend here," he pressed his lips to the dark, rough skin of the tentacle, "makes all of us believe that it's a technological marvel, a rig that's functioned, with minimal repair, for decades. It gives us more oil than any other rig, but it comes with a price. Can you guess what that is?"

Cameron moved his tongue as much as he could and lacerated it against his decimated teeth.

"That's right, it's humans." Sam smiled. "Now, since you're a clever bastard and can actually hear our ancient friend, I have been told to give you a choice. You can be a sacrifice and ensure the rig runs smoothly for another month. Or, you can join me, be its eyes and ears. It will pick out the sacrifice, and we must bring them here, to sustain our friend." Sam's grin seemed too wide all of a sudden. "What's it to be?"

With the last of his strength, Cameron wrapped his fingers around a pillar candle. "Go fuck yourself," he managed to spit out, and threw the candle in Sam's face. Sam screamed and reared up. The tentacles shuddered and a squeal, like metal grinding against metal, flooded Cameron's senses. Sam staggered and then fell through the hole.

Cameron couldn't move. He was going to die here. The certainty of it flooded him with peace. He closed his eyes and let his body relax. Eventually, the pain would fade. Without doubt, the throbbing in his head would subside. He longed for it.

Agony erupted through him as his body was lifted and cradled safely by what felt like a large snake. Cameron tried to fight, but the tentacles held him in a firm yet gentle grip. The howl of the sea grew louder, saltwater stung his cuts, and then he sank below the waves.

LOOK AT ME!

Cameron forced his eyes to open. Before him loomed a huge green eye. His battered body was reflected back at him in its vertical pupil.

DID YOU THINK IT WOULD BE THAT EASY? KILL MY CONNECTION AND I'D GO AWAY? YOU ANCHORED THIS MONSTROSITY INTO MY BODY. I CAN'T GO AWAY! AND NOW,

AS PENANCE FOR WHAT YOU HAVE DONE, YOU WILL TAKE HIS PLACE.

The tentacles wrapped around his arms then sank into his skin, leaving permanent, tattoo-like marks of their likeness.

YOU WILL BE MY EYES. YOU WILL BE MY EARS. YOU WILL NEVER BE ALONE AGAIN AS I WILL ALWAYS BE IN YOUR HEAD. YOU WILL NEVER LEAVE THE RIG, BUT THE ILLUSION WILL NOT AFFECT YOU, AND EVERY MONTH YOU WILL BRING ME A HUMAN I PICK. A FITTING SACRIFICE.

IF YOU REFUSE THIS PAYMENT, I WILL DESTROY THE RIG, TAKING EVERY SOUL DOWN WITH IT. AND WHILE YOU MAY THINK THERE'RE VERY FEW REAL PEOPLE ON THIS PLATFORM, REMEMBER, YOU CAME HERE IN A FULL HELICOPTER. ARE YOU WILLING TO LET HUNDREDS DIE TO SAVE ONE?

Cameron opened his mouth and seawater flooded his lungs. The stone skin of the tentacles raked at his flesh as they wrapped around his neck. Sickle-shaped claws sunk into his eyes.

YOU ARE MINE, LITTLE PRIMATE. SERVE YOUR GOD WITH LOVE.

Cameron's scream erupted in a plume of bloodied bubbles. Thick gobs of jelly oozed down his face, the remains of his eyes. In their absence, his brain burst into overdrive feeding him an array of violently colourful abstract pictures, then, through the confusion, a shape started to form.

Kelpie 5 was being dragged into place behind a huge ship. It gleamed in the sun. Its paintwork was spotless, it's rooms untouched. The legs were on a separate barge in two pieces. The ships reached their destination. Huge cranes hoisted one end of the first section of legs and slid them slowly into the blue-grey sea. Under the waves, a huge octopus-like creature slept. Its body was one with the rock and sand that made up the sea bed, it's granite hide studded with shells, anemone and seaweed. It rumbled peacefully as it slept, its gargantuan lungs heaving out one breath after another.

The legs hit the creature. Spikes carved into the feet drove deep into its flesh, sending ribbons of muscle and dark blue blood into the salt water. The monster bellowed and shook the ground with its roar. It conjured massive waves that threatened to topple the ships, but they stood firm. The next section of legs dropped, pinning the giant creature to the sea bed. It was losing too much blood. It was too weak to fight. All sorts of sea life swam to its aid but none could dislodge the metal that pierced its flesh. With a heaving, laboured breath, it grew still and its massive eye slowly closed.

Above the waves, Kelpie 5 was being fixed into position above its spindly legs. The teams celebrated, heedless to the destruction their prized rig had caused before it had even bored its first hole.

A few days later, Kelpie 5 went into full operation. A massive drill bored through the creature's body, waking it from its healing sleep. In rage, it wrapped its many tentacles around the legs of the rig and squeezed. With a scream, the metal buckled, and the whole rig tumbled into the sea.

Cameron saw many familiar faces floating in the sunken platform. Ben, Danny, Mary. Those who hadn't died in the initial fall fought to reach higher floors and hopefully the top deck, where they may have stood a chance in the open water, but no one escaped. Kelpie 5 hit the seabed near its destroyer. It was no longer a rig, but a mass grave.

The creature still couldn't escape, the legs held it fast. For a while, it fed itself with the bodies of the rig workers, but even the hundred drowned bodies didn't sustain it for long. Out of desperation, it hatched a plan. It resurrected the rig, and bound its injured body with the metal. It made likenesses of the dead crew out of its own flesh and parts of the rig, and used its powers to move them in a parody of their human lives. When the first crews came to salvage the rig, they found it not only standing, but functioning, with a crew one hundred strong pumping out oil.

The creature quickly grew weary of keeping the rig looking pristine. It flooded the air with its venom, a specialised neurotoxin that made its victims hallucinate. Every so often it plucked a worker from the deck, or through the holes in the lower floors, but it didn't always pick the best food, and found itself hungering again not long after eating. It needed to perfect its hunt.

From that first crew, the creature enslaved Sam. Sam could see through the illusion the monster had created with its body and toxins. Moments before he reported what he saw, the creature dragged him through the hole in the floor, beat him into submission, explained it's predicament, and then installed Sam on the rig as his eyes and ears. The ultimate lure. A befriender of the best potential food and the creature's one way of ensuring it got fed regularly. And in exchange for its sustenance, and to ensure a continuing supply, it gave the humans exactly what they wanted. Oil.

It had survived like that for years, taking one human a month, no one knowing, no one suspecting.

UNTIL YOU! The creature grumbled.

The vision ended, and Cameron slid into welcoming, warm darkness.

☠☠☠

The new recruits filed onto the rig. Cameron watched them sit at the decrepit tables under the rotted roof with its spider web trails of wires and gaping holes to the floor above. Every third person was nothing more than an illusion, a creation built from rusting metal and the ancient biology of the god beneath the waves. His own table was completely populated with imposters. They ate the putrid food from the cracked plates, drank stagnant water from shattered glasses, just like the human inhabitants did, and no one even suspected that something was amiss. No one knew that the very food they ate perpetuated the illusion of the functioning oil rig.

The poor idiots had no idea they were basically living in a gigantic Venus fly trap.

THAT ONE! The creature intoned into Cameron's skull. He felt his gaze being pulled towards a young roustabout with the olive skin and dark hair of someone born along the Mediterranean. *I FEEL LIKE TRYING SOMETHING EXOTIC.*

Cameron nodded in reply. He memorised the guy's features, then turned back to his untouched plate. He didn't eat anymore; he didn't have to know that he was nothing more than a zombie.

QUICKLY, the creature grumbled. *AND REMEMBER, IF YOU DO NOT FULFIL YOUR DUTY, I WILL DESTROY THIS PLACE ONCE MORE, AND RESURRECT IT WITHOUT YOU. YOU ARE AN INCONSEQUENTIAL PUPPET.*

Cameron sent his silent answer through his head. He would obey. It was dangerous to think otherwise.

He left the canteen and wandered under the hallway roof constructed of ugly grey skin pulled over vertebrae and ribs. The

102

doorways constantly moved. The rig trembled with the strain of pumping oil. It wouldn't survive a second resurrection. The years had put too much strain on it. Maybe all he had to do was bide his time.

A searing pain ripped through his brain. *DON'T BE NAIVE. AS LONG AS I AM STUCK HERE, I WILL FIND A WAY TO FEED.*

Cameron straightened up and shook his head to relieve the lingering pain. He reached out and patted the wall lovingly. "You will have what you need," he whispered. "I promise."

The metal of the wall bulged around his hand. It was as much of a response as he could expect. He wandered down into the bowels of the rig, carefully stepping over holes and trailing tentacles. This was his home now. And whether he liked it or not, he had to ensure it survived.

LIKE You

by Z Lee

Like You

You're all but a memory now; a tainted morsel of thought that pervades my subconscious and refuses to leave. I can't sleep. I'm kept awake by nightmares of you.

The sand was thick under my feet. Thousands of years of rock beaten upon by the sea had been reduced to tiny beads of silt between my toes. Twilight turned the waters black—a foreshadowing of your news. As you inhaled a shaky breath of nicotine and tar, you refused to look me in the eye.

I don't love you anymore, doll.

I'd reduced myself to skin pulled taut over bone for you. I'd starved myself and then conjured lies about the weakness in my knees. I dedicated every moment, of every day of my existence to make you happy. I changed in all the ways you demanded.

And then you said I wasn't the woman you knew.

That wasn't just the last night we spoke. It was the last night anyone ever saw you alive.

Fliers with your black and white devil's grin whipped in the wind and chased other bits of trash along the ground throughout town. Midnight vigils were held for you. It was the one party no one expected you at.

They didn't see what I saw—the monster that raged within. They never felt the stinging slaps or the breathless tunnel vision you forced on me. You ran my family and friends off with lies and hateful messages falsely addressed from me. Those strangers didn't lay next to you at night, counting the seconds between each of your breaths and praying the next would not come.

I did.

Still… I loved you once—long before years of extreme calorie counting withered me down to a defeated vole. Even as you sank

105

below the water, waving violently like a child's hearty goodbye, I loved you. With my toes dug deep in the sand, refusing to budge as you took your last breath, one hand over my mouth to keep my sobs and the chance of laughter from bubbling to the surface, I loved you.

I imagine your limbs tangled in a reef somewhere, hooked between rocks at unnatural angles and slowly growing coral over your bones. I like to think that the beautiful face that tricked me into a life I didn't want or deserve, is still beautiful in some way— providing a home for some manner of fish. I sit down in the sand and wonder if the minuscule beads of rock will one day grate away at my being, the way the salt of the sea grinds away yours.

I wonder what kind of person I have become; what kind of person I could have been. Who would you have hurt next? Would you have tried to take me back?

I come here often. Not just to reminisce, but because your death is still almost too good to be true.

Just like you.

BELOW THE BOAT

by Alexandra Englehart

Darling, my dearest darling,
What dense world is this?
We have found ourselves within
The deepest, darkest abyss.
Can you feel the pressure
As we float down, farther?
Is that your heartbeat
That's beginning to falter?
No sights, no sounds
In the spaces below us,
The breathless wreckage
And the stillness it touches.
Have you been to the bottom?
Have you ever felt this cold?
Are you ready for the silence?
Tell me, have we gotten old?
It's much too dark, I fear
We'll be lost within the night.
So too, this unyielding chill
Will remove us all from sight.

SEA OF SALT

by Elana Gomel

Kirsten is dead. Or perhaps she had never been born.

I met her when I came to campus for preliminary registration, still feeling awkward in civilian clothes. I literally bumped into her as I was backing out of the registration office, leafing through the hefty package of meaningless forms. She made a polite sound of protest: a sure indication that she was foreign. She looked foreign too, which accounted for my attraction. She was not pretty. Her peaky face was dominated by bulging eyes. Her large mouth looked squashed rather than sensuous. Her only truly attractive feature – or truly abhorrent, depending on your taste – was her milky-white skin, so uncompromisingly Aryan that the Mediterranean sunlight seemed to slide off her in defeat.

We sat on the grass while long-legged ibises stepped gingerly around us and went through the booklet of instructions together. I wish I could say that by this point we were at ease with each other, but it would be a lie. We were never at ease with each other.

But we did have coffee together and eventually I got invited into her room in the dorms. She worked so hard at being uninhibited that I felt more like a medical specimen than a lover. She told me she was going to study the history of the Jewish people. I felt I was demeaning myself in her eyes when I confessed my goal was business administration.

When we went out she would wear tight-fitting black dresses and a golden six-pointed star around her neck. She insisted I call her Avital and told me she wanted to convert. I laughed the first time I heard it. But she was impervious to hints or veiled insults. She took everything at face value. The stare of those pale eyes froze absurdities into horrible truths. Later my grandmother taught me the expression *tierischer Ernst:* bestial seriousness of the Germans.

After a while, we moved in together. She paid the rent with

her family money.

It was at this time that she started telling me about her grandfather. She told me his name on one of the few occasions our sex was truly passionate, whispered it like a love confession. It meant nothing to me. All I had gotten from the history lessons in school were cartoon images of waving flags and goose-stepping soldiers. And my grandparents never talked.

Now, of course, I know a lot about him, having read all I could lay my hands on. Some of those stories are stuck in my memory like bits of gristle between the teeth. He distributed sweets to the Gypsy children and they called him "Uncle." He would take his favorites for a ride in his car and sometimes drop them by the gas chamber. Once he gave his prisoner assistant – he called them "colleagues" and was invariably polite to them, especially to women – a box to prepare for delivery. She opened it: it was filled with human eyes.

The first semester was ending, and we were making plans for the winter break. I wanted to go to Germany with her, but she was reluctant. We quarreled, and I even accused her of being ashamed of me. I expected vehement denials, but she was silent. I stormed out; she called me ten minutes later and offered, as a gesture of reconciliation, to finance a long weekend at the Dead Sea.

James Joyce called the Dead Sea "the cunt of the world." Set inside the ring of ancient crumbling rocks, so old they have become soft and wistful, edging into mineral senility, the heavy-water lake called the Sea of Salt in Hebrew defies time. It is alive with a frightening concentrated vitality like the flow of a woman's juices: a doorway into the womb of the past.

We went spiraling down the new highway into the oldest place on Earth. The scanty vegetation was disappearing to reveal the baroquely shaped bones of the earth: pink, and scarlet, and dull bronze; elaborately folded and pleated; surrounded by aprons of scree. I felt loose as if the cord that bound me to everyday life was unraveling. I glanced at Kirsten; she looked inscrutable, gilded by the sunset.

On the shore the viscous water glistened beyond the wide stretch of salt flats. Ragged birds swooped over our heads. I still remember the tranquility of that moment.

We checked into the Nirvana hotel. Kirsten went straight to the spa. I walked down to the pebbly beach and touched the oily swell. Under the surface I could see white convoluted shapes like corals. They were salt crystals, growing in the sterile water in a perfect imitation of life. I heard the crunch of footsteps and turned around. Kirsten stood behind me, her white top luminescent in the dusk.

"I thought you were at the spa," I said.

"I like it better here."

We stood together in companionable silence.

"Is this where Lot's wife…?" she asked.

"Somewhere around," I shrugged. "A guided tour would show you the exact pillar of salt supposed to be her. Each tour has a different one."

We went back to the hotel, had a lavish dinner, and made love on the king-size bed. When I woke up in the middle of the night and found myself alone I thought she had simply moved over to the other side. Kirsten was never one for cuddling. But a quick glance told me she was not in bed. A longer investigation assured me she was not in the suite.

I was annoyed rather than concerned. Unable to fall asleep, I turned on the TV and watched a soft-porn film on the hotel's channel. Just as the moans of assorted male and female actors rose to a crescendo (they appeared to speak Turkish on the rare occasions they spoke at all), the door creaked and she walked in.

She was stark naked. In the ghostly TV light her skinny body glistened from head to toe, her hair lanky and wet. I stared. Did she go swimming in the Dead Sea in the middle of the night?

"Turn this filth off!" she yelled. And then she started sobbing.

She was covered in dirt mixed with oily water into a sort of paste. I took her to the bathroom and turned on the shower. The water swirling down the drain had a reddish tint.

Wrapped up in one of the hotel's huge towels, she swallowed a drink I thrust into her hand, pulling a bottle at random from the mini-bar. I was seized by panic, wondering whether she had gone off her head. Kirsten had always appeared to me insufferably self-possessed and such people have the capacity for sudden and spectacular breakdowns. Finally, she started talking.

"It wasn't like that at all," she said. "It was not supposed to be that way."

"What wasn't?" I asked.

"The place. I thought it would be cold. But it was hot, stifling. Summer, I thought. But there was no vegetation, nothing, just a field of ashes. Like the volcanic ash but heavier. Wasn't it supposed to be among the fields? I read about neighboring villages gathering their harvest just a couple of kilometers away. But there wasn't a spot of green I could see."

"There is no green here," I said stupidly.

"And the smell," she went on. "I knew there would be a smell but not like this. I thought it would smell like…like roast, like a joint in the oven."

Kirsten was a strict vegetarian; the cause of many a squabble when we ate out.

"But it wasn't. It was bitter, chemical, like toilet cleaner, only stronger. Disinfectant. What do they do with the bodies to make them smell like this?"

This was getting to be too much for a holiday weekend.

"What the fuck are you talking about?" I yelled. "Where have you been? What happened?"

I think my presence fully registered only then. She looked at me and smiled, almost tenderly.

"Poor Gilad," she said. "*Mein Süße.*"

I felt like slapping her face but then I saw something that made me gulp in horror. There was a dark spreading patch on the white terrycloth around her chest.

"You're bleeding," I said.

She looked down and lifted the towel. There was no wound. The blood was oozing from her nipples, pooling in the crease of her stomach. She made a face and swabbed it with the stained towel.

"I thought these puddles were sewage," she said.

I rushed into the bathroom and threw up. When I came back, Kirsten was in bed, asleep.

❀ ❀ ❀

I had dozed off on the couch and woke up, groggy, with the sound of the shower. When Kirsten came out, she seemed her usual self. I postponed serious talk until after breakfast. Then, fortified with black coffee, I told her we should go back immediately to seek medical help (I was careful not to say "psychiatric"). She smiled and shook her head. Despite the dark circles of fatigue under her eyes, she seemed elated.

"No," she said. "You go back if you want. I'm staying here. Perhaps I'll look for cheaper accommodations. I don't know how long it'll take."

"How long will what take?" I shouted.

"I'm going to find him," she said.

☠ ☠ ☠

The Dead Sea and its environs are crawling with Mediterranean history. There are Sodom and Masada; there are remnants of Roman fortifications; there are abandoned bunkers of the Jordanian army. If the past were to invade the present here, why should it be that alien European past, the graveyard stench of Poland, the war madness of Germany?

But she did go somewhere. I saw it myself. I saw her walk into the heavy water that parted before her like some colossal ameba, the smooth flanks of the sea drawing in upon themselves as she stood on the oily shingles. It was as if she covered an immense distance with each step, visibly shrinking, becoming the size of a child, a toddler, a doll. There was a silver flash as she vanished into somewhere else and the roiling water resumed its normal appearance.

She swore to me there was no magic formula. All she had to do was to visualize the tunnel of light. At the time I did not know what she was talking about. Since then, I have read books on out-of-the-body experiences: people who float up a heavenly rabbit hole to meet their dear departed or have a chat with Jesus. It's easy if you know how.

But wherever she went, it was not to heaven. She was convinced – at least, at the beginning – she had found a door to the past. I quickly realized it was not. But I did not know what brave new world she discovered in the depth of her guilt. That world reached out and devoured her; that much was certain. But was it merely her own nightmare? Was I just a bystander, innocently caught in the turbulence of her family history? I pretended to believe it then; I don't pretend now.

Perhaps the pretense was thin even then for the fact is, I did

113

not run away. We moved into a bungalow in a holiday village: cheaper and more private. We developed a daily routine that was almost cozy in its insanity. The horror only came back occasionally. One morning, looking down into the pink *wadi*, I saw a herd of gazelles pass by so close I could touch them. They walked in a single file and as they passed the fenced overhang where I stood, each of them stopped and looked at me.

After breakfast we would drive down to the sea, seeking a secluded place. It was not easy because the shore is as flat as a pancake. There are no bays or coves. But we counted on indifference. If a passing driver got a glimpse of Kirsten's white buttocks, so what? There is no law saying you cannot go skinny-dipping in the Dead Sea. She insisted on going in naked because this is how it worked for her the first time. But since the time of the day was not affected by her passage, she did not want to go at night. She needed daylight: to see, to observe, to witness.

But witnessing was tricky because it changed every time she went there. The basic outline was the same: a field of ashes; a sullen sky that ran the gamut from fire-gray to crimson; and the watchtowers on the horizon. Those spidery black silhouettes, she was convinced, marked the camp where he was waiting for her. On the first visits she did not manage to come close enough to make out the gates because assorted obstacles barred her way. It was the variety of these obstacles that made me realize she could not simply journey into the past. Sometimes the wasteland would be cut by trenches, filled with skeletons in tattered uniforms like World War I soldiers felled by a cloud of gas. Sometimes she encountered a maze of ravines threaded with foul-smelling streams that built up dams of human excrement. And once the plain was alive with tiny lemming-like rodents that scrambled and fought, rising tiny plumes of ash.

The length of her visits also varied; occasionally she would come out in twenty minutes, faint with hunger, and claim to have spent a whole day there. Other times I had to wait until the moonrise to hear the crunch of her footsteps on salt crystals.   I fed her and tried to do something about the stigmata of her journey, mostly with no success. And then I would debrief her. This is how I called it to myself as if I was still in Lebanon. I tried to record her but she refused. So I bought a notepad in the holiday village's souvenir shop and wrote it all down in longhand.

On her fourth journey, she said, she saw a line of prisoners weaving among the hillocks of cinders and stretches of black porous stone that comprised the landscape around the camp. She hid behind the rusty ruin of some agricultural machinery; or perhaps it was a military truck. She was vague about such details. She was very precise about the prisoners and their guards, however.

The prisoners, she said, were both men and women. There were no children. They were horribly emaciated, the striped rags of their uniforms barely covering the skeletal bodies but even this scanty covering was almost too much for the stifling heat of that place, the boiling air reeking with sulfur and acid fumes. Some of them, even women, pulled off the shirts, baring the torso in a vain attempt to escape the heat. The guards did not interfere because the most important part of the outfit was impossible to remove. The yellow patches stuck to the prisoners' bare skin; mostly on the chest but sometimes on the forearm, the upper thigh, the shaven head or even covering most of the face. The patches stood out in relief, as thick as a man's hand: not merely a swatch of cloth but a plump padded thing. The patches seemed to her to twitch and change shape. She wanted to come closer but was afraid of the guards.

"They were not human," she said.

"Sure," I said sarcastically, "make them into monsters so we don't have to accept that we are all capable of cruelty."

"I don't mean metaphorically," she said impatiently. "I mean they were something else."

They wore immaculate black uniforms. But unlike in the familiar movies, they also had shiny black helmets that covered the entire face.

"Like medieval knights?" I asked dubiously.

"Yeah, only medieval helmets are very elaborate, with moving parts. These were completely featureless, a sort of hemisphere with a thick curving edge that sat on the shoulders."

"How did they breathe?"

"I don't know."

But what made her believe the guards were not quite human was the way they moved, slinking with a boneless grace around the stumbling column of prisoners. And then there was the way they killed.

"She stumbled and fell, this woman. I think she was a young

girl but ages were difficult to tell. She tried to get up but a guard approached, flipped her over with the tip of his boot, and ground his foot into her chest. She wailed and thrashed but he kept on and his foot actually sunk into her body as if it were made of rotting cheese. Blood jetted out but I think – I could not be sure – that it slid off his uniform like water off a duck's back. A couple of other guards joined him and one of them bent and tore off the woman's arm – just tore it off, with no visible effort, twirled it in the air and threw it away. It landed not very far from me and it was... it was a *real* arm, real flesh and blood, because when he did this I thought, it can't be, these people are not real, they are puppets or simulations, nobody can pull a human body apart like a paper doll. But they did. And the rest of the prisoners watched."

⚜ ⚜ ⚜

Several times I wanted to call a doctor. I could not be responsible for what was happening to her. And I admit, I was squeamish.

But at the end I did not. I gave in. I became her assistant, chronicler, witness, and nurse. I obeyed her orders. She had this effect on me. Without love, without gratitude, commitment or obligation, she bound me to herself more securely than any other woman before or since.

Her nipples did not bleed after the first time. But when she crawled out of the sea for the second time and stood shivering as I threw a robe around her, I noticed angry red stripes on her back. The skin was puffy, as if she had been lashed with a belt.

"What is this?" I asked.

She shrugged.

"Does it hurt?"

"A little," she said reluctantly. I put some aloe gel on her back and tried to pretend it was the effect of the seawater. But the third time she came back with half her hair torn out by the roots, the bare patches on her scalp raw and bleeding. She cut off the remnant of her hair and shaved her head with my electric shaver. Were it not for the scabs, it might even have suited her.

I thought that perhaps she had been discovered. I imagined her naked figure crawling in the ashes. Had she been gang-raped? I was

116

afraid to ask. But that night she pushed herself against me with a startling desperation and we made love like two castaways on some bleak shore. This was the last time; when she returned the next day, she tried to hide her body from me but I could see how her journey had marked her. More than mere mutilation, it was as if her flesh had melted in the passage and then cooled into a ragged new shape. After that, she came back every time with a new brand, like notches on a gun to mark the killings.

She did not mind; she was preoccupied with more practical concerns. She wanted to spy on the camp. She was upset because she had not managed to approach it any closer: her way had been blocked by a giant pile of discarded clothing, suitcases, shoes, toys, all mixed together and dumped in the midst of the wasteland. Rooting in it, she found a teenager's pants and a man's khaki shirt that fit her, dug a little hole and hid the clothes, marking the site with a rock. Next time she would snoop around properly dressed in dead people's hand-me-downs. I was struck by the gruesome irony of it, but she was not; rather, she was puzzled by the seeming senselessness of the dump.

She could not understand the economic logic of the camp, she said. I laughed when she first talked about it. But then I began to realize she was serious. She had to come to terms with the camp with by squeezing it into the procrustean bed of her rationality. She was not content to turn away in disgust from the meaninglessness of atrocity; she had to force atrocity to make sense and then she could live with it. It made her abhorrent in my eyes; it made her admirable; and as distant as if we were denizens of different galaxies.

The prisoners were often marched around the camp, going nowhere. To me, it sounded familiar, almost mundane; there were the death marches after the camps had to be evacuated and the purpose of these marches was killing, pure and simple. This camp, however, seemed in no danger of liberation as there were no signs of war around it; no drone of warplanes or distant rumbling of the artillery. There were crematoria inside and they worked at full capacity. She saw the tall chimneys protruding into the yellow air, belching oily smoke and an occasional tongue of flame. Even the sickening stench of the burnt human flesh that she had missed on the first occasion was there, only masked by the piercing odor of unknown chemicals. So, she insisted, there was no point to those impromptu death marches.

"Perhaps the gas chambers and crematoria are overloaded," I suggested.

It was possible, she agreed reluctantly. There was a railway line that brought prisoners in: occasionally she could see a tiny train on the horizon. Still, there was something about the killings that puzzled her. When she came back after her fifth visit eager and excited, I knew she had solved the mystery.

"I know now!" she exclaimed.

She came across a heap of dead bodies, not very large, perhaps twenty people in all. Most seem to have died of sheer exhaustion; several were shot. The bodies were stacked together like firewood. Approaching them cautiously, trying not to breathe in the death-stink, she saw stirrings in the heap. She thought of rats; but the creature that wriggled out and plopped onto the cindery ground resembled a starfish. It was poisonous yellow, with a rough tegument and six radial arms that it proceeded to flex as it flopped around.

"Those patches," she explained, "are not sewed-on pieces of fabric but living organisms. They are parasites, feeding on the prisoners. I think that they need dead bodies for the incubators. This is why a certain percentage of prisoners are not burnt but killed outside the camp. I saw groups of inmates on the plain before, moving from one pile of bodies to another. I thought they were *Sondercommando*. But now I believe they were harvesting the stars."

I stared at her. There is a threshold in horror beyond which lies sheer numbness and a kind of detached curiosity. I was at this stage but she – she was somewhere else. Her cheeks were flushed.

"Where do you think these creatures come from?" I asked.

"I think they've been made in the camp," she replied. "I think…" she hesitated slightly, "I think *he* made them."

Next time she came close enough to the gates to see the familiar inscription *Arbeit macht frei*. She was relieved; she had heard a prisoner scream something in a language she did not understand and was concerned about the possibility of miscommunication. This was also the first time she saw the guard dogs. They were large sleek brutes with naked pink paws like rats and semi-human faces, pug-nosed and slit-eyed. She was convinced they talked to the prisoners.

She refused to let me tend to herself but when she fell asleep I saw a pink growth, like a fleshy coral, on her thorax. I lay down on the couch, revolted and hating myself for my revulsion.

How to get into the camp? That was the problem she pondered incessantly.

"Most inmates wonder how to get out," I said sarcastically. She just shrugged but I began to consider whether this was true, whether there was, in fact, any place to get out to. It seemed to me that her stories of the camp world were growing more bizarre, more hellishly elaborate, as if that world was diverging further from our knowledge of the past. Perhaps by now there was no war, no opposition to the camp system, and no hope for the people who were used as hatcheries for monsters.

"There is a camp ecology I have to understand," she said. "The yellow stars I think are just larvae. Perhaps at the next stage they become the guard-dogs."

"What for?" I asked.

"I read his diaries," she said. "He really believed in what he was doing. He was a scientist, not a butcher. Perhaps here he has the chance to put his theories into practice. Perhaps in that world they are *true.*"

"How do you know he even exists in that world?" I asked.

"Oh, I know," she said unhesitatingly. "He's there, I can feel him. This is why…" she added after a while, in that contemplative tone that always gave me the chills, "this is why it all looks so familiar."

"Why don't you just walk to the gate, then, and say you have come for a family visit?" I asked.

She looked at me with those bulging eyes. Her face by now had the uncompromising look of a martyr.

"If I don't find any other way, I will do it," she said.

"I want to come with you," I said.

"No."

Of course, I could have argued. I could have followed her.

I did neither.

The last time I waited for her for the entire day. The brief violet dusk came and went, and she was not back. I prowled the edge of the sea; the sounds of singing and laughter came from the new promenade.

Exhausted, I drove back to the bungalow. When I saw the light streaming from the windows I almost crashed the car.

Kirsten was inside, sitting on the bed, her head in her hands. She had put some clothes on but there was black water pooling at her feet.

"I've seen him," she said.

"How did you get here?" I yelled.

"I walked," she said vaguely. "Listen, I've seen him."

I don't believe she had walked up half a mile, naked and barefoot, from the shore to the bungalow. I suspect the worlds were bleeding into each other and she was the wound, the raw place where they rubbed. Her mutilations were signs of their contact; and the wider the zone of contact became, the more randomly was she tossed along the edge.

Apparently, she had taken my advice. She had simply walked to the camp entrance and announced herself. I imagine her standing at the bottom of the curving ramp, a tiny figure in the wasteland of ashes and poison, looking up at the towering ironwork of the gate.

Her description of the camp was rather vague but also surprisingly prosaic: prosaic, that is, in the sense that it was not all that different from the descriptions I have read since then in historical books. She talked about the barbed wire, the churned-up bare earth, rows of barracks, smell of excrement. Not too many inmates were around. Those she saw were shuffling *Musslemen*, living skeletons with extinguished eyes covered in filth and sores. They, however, were free of yellow stars, confirming her hunch that the creatures were parasites that needed relatively healthy hosts. The guards who escorted her did not speak and seeing them from close up, she decided they could not. The helmets were actually their real heads, covered with a shining black carapace like a beetle-wing. She tried to figure out how they fed and came to the conclusion that they had mouths in the palms of their hands. She was convinced now that the guard-dogs were their masters.

Brought to the medical barrack – she caught a glimpse of a room filled with small cots, a child in each – she was led into an office. There was a desk with a typewriter, a fringed Art Deco lamp, and a portrait on the wall. Not the familiar face with a tiny mustache. Not a human face at all.

She was left waiting in the company of a nurse, a youngish woman in a starched uniform. She refused to talk but gave Kirsten a sugar cube. And then her grandfather walked in.

They talked. There were no spy-novel attempts at disguise; she did not pretend to be a special envoy from Berlin. She told him she was his descendant from the future; she said she had traveled back in time. He was familiar with the concept; being an educated man, he had read H. G. Wells. However – and this indicates to me he had realized there was something fishy about the situation – he did not ask her many questions about the future, though he did inquire about his family. Instead, he seemed to be only too pleased to talk about his work in the camp.

It was, as she had suspected, an attempt to create a total ecology of death, in which the energy released by torture and extermination would be used to promote the malleability of the living flesh.

"Think about it as a fountain of youth, like the legendary spring of Eldorado," he had said enthusiastically. "There is no limit to improvements we can achieve. Total freedom from disease, physical perfection, mental acuity, all fertility problems solved once and for all."

The yellow starfish, the black-helmeted guards, and the talking guard-dogs were just experiments, she gathered (inside the camp, most personnel seemed ordinary enough but on her way out she caught a glimpse of a creature like a giant dun-colored caterpillar crawling on two rows of human hands). The prisoners were vermin whose extermination was a necessary hygienic precaution; it was the greatest boon to science that this simple public-health measure also opened a window of opportunity for the human race.

What else had passed between them at this family reunion, I wonder. What else was said, perhaps not in words but in exchange of looks, in the body language? She had spent her entire life in his shadow, thinking and dreaming of him, hating him, but perhaps also admiring his courage in stepping outside the bounds of the merely human. All she had ever wanted, she told me, was to separate herself from him. But is it really possible? The more she looked into the past that should have been dead but wasn't, the more the past looked back at her. The past had reshaped her in its image even before she took off her clothes that evening. Her white skin was festooned with hanging sacs of skin filled with milky liquid and there was a tiny dark core in each, a fetus-like form turning head over heels.

"I am going back tomorrow," she said. "I am going to kill him. You are a soldier; you will teach me how."

I took her with me, bundled in layers of my T-shirts, as we sped on the empty highway. It was pretty late to come knocking at the door, but the owner of the flat-roofed house in a small village owed me a favor. Arms are easy to come by in a country at war. The handgun could be hidden under her clothes. All she had to do was pull the trigger.

We were back at the Dead Sea just as the first rays of the sun broke over the Jordanian hills, turning the heavy water into a sheet of beaten gold. In that glorious light Kirsten's wasted skull-like face looked frightful. And yet I felt something close to adoration as I looked at her. We both knew she was not coming back. Heroism is the opium of fools.

I tried to postpone the moment, offering her coffee, keeping up the feeble pretence of normality. She refused and tucking the gun, carefully wrapped in a plastic bag, inside the waistband of her pants, walked to the sea edge. It occurred to me that it was the first time she was going to cross dressed.

I watched her as she paused with her feet planted in the viscid swell. I hoped she would look back at me. But she did not and I realized, once again, how little I meant to her. It had been between him and her all along.

She started walking in and the sea parted as usual. But something was different; there was angry churning and the water, normally so sluggish, rose in foamy billows that twisted as if whipped by a gale, even though the air was still. A piercing whistle assaulted my ears, rising to an unendurable pitch as the sea exploded into a harsh blaze. I fell down. Groveling on the ground, my eyes watering from the Hiroshima radiance that turned the flying foam into the hail of fire, I could still see Kirsten's dark silhouette. She must have screamed but her voice was drowned in the rage of the Dead Sea, offended at her presumption in carrying an instrument of death into its domain. I could see the metallic glitter of the sky through her body as the waves dissolved her flesh, eating holes in legs, buttocks, and thighs. An especially large wave broke over her and when it retreated a pristine skeleton was standing in the sea, its arms still raised in supplication. But the sea was already giving it new flesh, covering the slender bones with the coat of interlocking crystals that grew into a structure of surpassing beauty, as lacy and delicate as the rime patterns on the windowpane. This new creation, however, endured for an even shorter time than Kirsten's own fragile body, for the salt statue broke up and fell into the hungry water that swallowed it up and buried it in its own salty depth.

❦ ❦ ❦

It has been ten years. I don't remember the days that followed but eventually the routine won, as it always does. I called her parents and told them their daughter had left me, but I did not think she would be coming home soon. They were not surprised.

I make good money. I am married and have a three-year-old daughter. When she was born, I wanted to call her Kirsten. My wife was shocked by the idea. We called her Shirley.

Recently I took a day off work and drove down to the Dead Sea. I walked on the promenade in the pale silvery light of the late afternoon. A boy was sitting on the parapet, reading a book, resting his feet on his huge backpack. He was blond and blue-eyed. As I approached, he lifted his head and smiled at me.

"U.S.?" I asked as I sat down beside him.

"Germany," he replied.

We chatted a little. His life was brand-new, untarnished by memory. He was highly complimentary about my command of Deutsch.

"History is a nightmare from which I am trying to awaken," said Joyce. But what if a nightmare becomes history? I imagine Kirsten and myself yoked together by elastic bonds that warp out of shape as they stretch back in time but never snap. Unless they are cut.

My wife kids me for working out so obsessively. But I have to be in top shape when I'm ready to cross the Sea of Salt and enter the undead past in order to put it to rest.

I will be ready soon.

THE THING IN THE WATER

by Carla E. Dash

The thing in the water started singing to me after Lizet died.

I bought the kitten from a shelter on a lark when Marion and the kids moved out. There was nothing wrong with the cat; she was just one too many. Someone, somewhere didn't spay their pet, and then, when she fell pregnant and birthed her kits, this someone thought: *this creature, this life my actions allowed to enter to the world, I don't want it, we don't have enough room, we can't afford it, it'd be an inconvenience.* So they abandoned her in a sad little cage in the back of a shelter.

I spent a month with Lizet, scratching behind her fluffy ears and rolling her in the palms of my hands. She liked to sprint across the backyard, and she never tried to bolt for the street, so I started taking her for walks around the neighborhood. She stuck close to me, dancing circles around my feet.

One day, I brought her to the beach. She pawed the moist ground, trilling happily. Damp grains of sand stuck in the spaces between her pinprick claws. I didn't think she'd go for the water. You know, cat, water.

At first, it was funny watching her struggle in the waves. I didn't think she would have trouble getting out. Animals can all swim, can't they? It's a survival thing. I thought she was doing it awkwardly because she was so little and it was her first time. I didn't know she was in any danger. But when she sunk under and didn't come up, I stopped laughing.

I dove in with my clothes on, winter and all. The cold bit my flesh and the murk obscured by vision, but I found her, eventually. I wish I hadn't. Back on the shore, I cradled her wet, limp body in my hands, and sobbed like baby. She had been my responsibility. I had loved her. And now she was dead.

I didn't know what to do with the body. I panicked. I threw it back into the sea.

I didn't handle it well. I'd see a cat napping in a window as I passed, and I'd want to break the glass. Children darted across streets without looking, and I had to refrain from grabbing them by the shoulders and shaking them until their teeth clacked. I balled my fists, suppressing the urge to throttle parents at parks on cellphones, parents jaywalking with little fingers curled in theirs, parents smoking with one hand and pushing strollers with the other.

Anger. I was full of it. But I knew it, and I was coping. The singing was something else.

I kept hearing it along the paved pathway beside the beach on my way to the bus stop in the mornings and on the way home in the evenings. At first it barely registered, just a scrap of song wafting out of someone's window. A kid humming, maybe. Or someone practicing an instrument. Background noise in a city.

But it was always exactly the same melody. *La, la, la, la.* A regular pounding, like a knock on a door. Or footsteps. Or waves. It was too precise to be human. And then I realized there were words in the song, and the words were for me.

"Jay," came the whisper-song, in a clear, high voice, like the clang of a key on a kid's xylophone. That was it. Just my name, over and over. *Jay, Jay. Jay, Jay.*

I thought I was imagining it. I thought I was going out of my mind. I tapped the volume on my cell phone to the point of pain and ignored it.

But then I started hearing it in bed at night and at work during the day, on the assembly line between bolts. *Jay, Jay. Jay, Jay, Jay.*

One day, a little girl sat cross-legged on the path. She had dark hair, stormy eyes, and skin that looked hungry for the sun. Something about the structure of her face reminded me of Aria, my daughter, though I couldn't put my finger on what feature it was exactly that convinced me of the resemblance.

"Jay," she said.

I pulled the earbuds from my ears. "Sorry," I said. "Do I know you?"

"Jay," she said, standing. "Thank you for my kitty."

"What?" I said. I looked around, but no one was there to grin or laugh, to point or take pictures of the look on my face. But who would be? I hadn't told anyone about Lizet.

The nearest traffic light flicked from red to green, and cars drove through. A man banged the button for the crosswalk. Two underdressed teenagers edged too close to the curb and rolled their eyes at him. Everything was normal.

"Momma said I had to give it back, but I hung on and screamed until Momma gave in. She always gives in, eventually. Thank you for sending her. I was so lonely before, all by myself, with no one to play with."

I clutched the strap of my messenger bag, trying to get a grip. I'd jumped to a nutso conclusion, that's all. It was all a misunderstanding. "What cat?" I asked.

The girl tilted her head as if listening to a far off voice. "Lizet. What a beautiful name you gave her. Will you give me a name, too?"

"Look," I said. "I need to get going." I started walking, but the girl didn't move. I veered around her. She spun, to face me, but didn't follow. I felt her gaze on the back of my head.

"Do you know what I would really like?" she called at my back.

I shoved the earbuds back into my ears.

I went about my night. I lifted weights in the gym under my apartment. I nuked leftovers in the microwave and ate them in front of the TV. I answered emails. I double checked that I'd put in the right days for time off so that my schedule would be clear for Aria's visit. I slid under the sheets.

But I couldn't sleep. The thing with the little girl's face sang to me, asking me, begging me—*Jay, Jay*—for the thing that all only children want most of all, more even than a kitten.

A WINTER CROSSING

by Lynda Clark

There were cannibal rats on Rathburn. Or so the legend goes.

Roger's eyes had gone wide at the story and Carrie immediately regretted telling it. She was regretting it all the more now.

As the binoculars were dutifully placed in her outstretched hand, she glanced at Roger. The lad chewed a piece of loose skin from the edge of his fingernail and looked from the sea to Carrie and back again with large, worried eyes. Sighing, she raised the binoculars.

The waves looked like crumpled tinfoil, silvered peaks throwing up the grey light of the dying sun. Something bobbed in the distance, something pinkish and vaguely spherical.

"You talking about that buoy over there?"

"It wasn't a buoy!"

"Fine." Carrie tossed the binoculars back to her crewmate. "It was a severed head. Want to take the rowboat out and investigate?"

"Forget it." He turned away from the railings. "Tea?"

She nodded her approval and while Roger disappeared below decks, Carrie leaned on the railings and looked out to the bleak white horizon.

Cannibal rats might be pushing it, but in winter Rathburn wasn't much of a holiday destination, that was for sure. Once-sunny beaches turned to bleak stretches of slate, winds howling around the ruined castle. The castle where all the rat bones were found. In the legend.

During these long, cold months, MS *Rosenberg*'s job was to load up with food and supplies for the few resident islanders eking out a remote existence. Islanders like Roger's family, who ran the only tavern and arranged accommodation for summer visitors. Carrie shook her head. How could an island boy get so rattled by a few silly stories? Carrie loved that island and she hadn't even grown up there.

"Captain Roberts?" Roger's voice was muffled, coming from the small kitchen below deck.

Carrie watched a kittiwake bobbing on the waves a few metres away.

"What?"

The seabird rode the neaps, ducking its head under the water every few moments, sometimes coming up with a small silver fish dangling from its beak, sometimes with nothing.

"Where did you put everything?"

A dark shape, probably a seal, appeared beneath the kittiwake and circled slowly just beneath the surface.

"What everything? I didn't put anything anywhere!"

"The tea, the coffee, the bread, the tins, it's all gone!" Roger's voice rose, getting louder and more panicked with every word. Carrie could picture him crashing about in the tiny kitchen like a deranged cow, slamming the cupboards and throwing the contents all over.

"Hell's teeth!" Carrie headed for the stairs, her back to the kittiwake, which finally noticed its circling admirer and peered down into the water. It withdrew its head abruptly, letting out a loud squawk and flapping its wings to make a hasty getaway.

Carrie joined Roger in the kitchen and found him half buried in the cupboard under the sink, digging around in the bucket of cleaning products.

"You're not going to find tea in there, are you?"

Roger scuttled backwards and slammed the door shut, getting to his feet.

"Someone else is onboard."

"Yes, Roger, there's Moss."

"Apart from you, me and Moss!" Roger snapped.

Carrie softened. Roger seldom had a harsh word for anyone.

"Maybe Moss forgot to restock," she said gently, patting Roger's shoulder, "Let's go and ask him."

Moss and Carrie had worked the *Rosenberg* together for thirty years. If anyone had forgotten to restock the kitchen, it was Roger, but Carrie wasn't about to go pointing the finger right now. They'd be docking at Rathburn in an hour, for crying out loud, they could all cope without tea and biscuits for an hour.

Propelling Roger forward, her hand still on the lad's shoulder, Carrie headed back to the small navigation room at the front of the ship.

"Moss, would y-" the words died on her lips. Moss wasn't there. His florescent jacket lay on the floor beside the ship's control panel. The autopilot was engaged, but in these unpredictable winter seas, Moss liked to keep an eye on things in case the human touch was needed.

"Probably stepped out to pee," Carrie said with more certainty than she felt. She finally let go of Roger and nudged Moss's jacket with her toe. His walkie talkie lay on top of it. As Carrie stooped to pick it up, there was a loud yell and a splash from the deck.

"Moss!"

Roger was out the door so quickly it made Carrie's bones hurt just to think of moving at such speed.

"He's gone," said Roger quietly as Carrie joined him on deck.

"Don't be ridiculous Roger, damn fool probably fell in pissing over the side." Although the odds of an old seadog like Moss overbalancing on a day still as this was close to zero.

At least it had been still. Now, the water churned, like Moss was thrashing just below the surface, but couldn't break through. It made sense – he was a strong swimmer, but the water was cold, freezing. The shock of it would make it a trial to do anything other than splash. Even if he wasn't wearing a life jacket, it's not as if he'd just sink like a stone.

"I'll get the rowboat. He'll freeze to death in there."

"I'll go," Roger offered.

"No, no," Carrie waved him away, already unlashing the boat from where it was stowed. "You get on the radio and contact the coastguard."

Carrie heard Roger's sharp intake of breath and turned towards him. He was shaking, head darting left and right like a startled animal.

"Saw something!"

"What?"

"Something just leapt onto the boat! I saw it!"

"Roger," Carrie put a little of the old sea captain into her voice. "Stop scaring yourself and contact the coastguard."

"No," said Roger. "There's something on the boat. It was big and dark green. I saw it!"

He stepped past Carrie and snatched the rowboat, yanking it down onto the deck with a strength born of fear. He pulled his lifejacket tighter, lowered the boat over the edge and clambered down after it.

"I'll get Moss," he called up. "You get rid of that *thing* and call the coastguard!"

"There is no *thing*!" Carrie yelled after him, her temper finally getting the better of her.

And then she saw it. Not in the boat, but in the water, a dark shape lurking alongside Roger's oars.

"Roger," she called down, although the young man was already pulling away, his long, practised strokes fighting the roiling water. "Mind out – there's a seal near you. Watch he doesn't capsize you!"

Roger stopped rowing for a moment, cupped a hand to his ear to show he hadn't heard. Carrie was about to repeat herself when she noticed a thick fog had rolled in all around them, deadening all sound. The sea, seconds ago a boiling froth of motion, was now like a sheet of glass. The kind of silence you hear when something gets stuck in your throat. Long seconds where you can't breathe and the world stops.

A splash broke the silence, and things moved so fast, Carrie couldn't take in what happened. The seal leapt clear of the water, crashing into the rowboat, Roger yelled, the wood of the rowboat cracked and Roger disappeared beneath the surface.

Carrie gripped the railings, staring into the water, rooted to the spot. Roger should have surfaced by now. He was wearing a life jacket, if the cold overwhelmed him and he couldn't paddle, he should bob to the top like a buoy. Seals weren't usually aggressive outside breeding season, just misguidedly playful. Even if it dragged him beneath the surface, it would've let go by now.

She hurried to the radio to call the coastguard, trying to slow down what had happened, to replay it, but it was all too fast. A couple of ideas nagged at her, though. The 'thing'—she hated to call it that—was too long and lean to be a seal. It moved more like a dolphin, arcing through the water, but its dark green scaled hide ruled that ou-

Carrie stopped dead in the control room doorway. The radio was smashed and smoking, wires and circuit boards exposed. Its casing was cracked as if someone hit it with an axe. Moss's coat still lay on the floor, but now it was wet. There was water everywhere, all over the floor, dripping off the radio.

Radio.

Carrie stooped and felt around in Moss's jacket. The walkie talkie was still there. She exhaled slowly.

Not far to Rathburn. Just change the frequency on this thing and contact the lighthouse.

Carrie focused on the walkie talkie, virtually devoid of buttons and switches and wondered how the hell to make the damn thing work. Every time she pushed the transmit button, the radio crackled and hissed. Goddamnit, Roger always sorted the technical stuff. It was the only thing he was good at, the whole reason they had him on b-

The blow hit her full in the back and she could do little to stop her face smacking against the deck with a loud crack. Her first thought was pirates, although even as she thought it, it struck her as odd they'd bother with the *Rosenberg*. Stealing a rusty motor ship didn't seem right.

And then, after she'd been pinned a few seconds, there was sniffing close to her neck and the stench of rotting seaweed. Bile rose in her throat and without thinking she jerked an elbow loose and jabbed her attacker in the ribs. The creature—and creature did not seem like such a foolish word—issued a sound. It was an ancient, alien shriek. Carrie was up and running before she'd even thought about it, ignoring the throb of her arthritic joints.

Out on the deck she looked back. Through swimming vision and teary eyes from the blow to her head, she made out a dark humanoid shape, a glint of teeth and claws. All the encouragement she needed to dive from the prow and reach desperately for the floating remnants of the row boat with long, jagged strokes.

Gasping for breath, expecting needle teeth to clamp around her leg any second, her shaking fingers closed around a plank of driftwood and she let her chin drop onto the solid surface.

She came around when the cold bit into her bones. She wasn't sure how long she'd been out, strained to lift her head, craned her neck for a land mark.

And there it was, portside, the craggy lump of Rathburn Island. She was almost into the bay. If she could make-

Something moved on Rathburn Hill, a flash of midnight green. She closed her eyes. Cormorants, glossy feathers reflecting the green of the ocean below. Nothing more.

Unbidden, the old name for Rathburn popped into her head. Ratbone. The story she'd told Roger a lifetime ago: a colony of rats had swum to the island from a sinking ship in the eighteen hundreds. With no natural predators, the rats thrived and the colony grew and grew until-

Shaking her head, Carrie fought down the growing dread that she'd forever be trapped between the things in the sea and the things on the island. She kicked out, using her waning strength to power towards the bay.

The tide was coming in and aided her journey, although the current was washing her towards the cave set into the side of Rathburn Hill. She didn't want to go in there, but lacked the strength to steer back towards the rocky beach. As she neared the cave mouth, she saw them. Dark shapes perched in every nook. As the darkness swallowed her, she closed her eyes and longed to reach the other side. Cormorants? Creatures? No, it was just her mind playing tricks on her, making a monster of every shape and shadow. Although when she reached the island proper? Now that's a different story.

So the legend goes.

DARK WATER

by Lillian Csernica

I'd been working in the parking kiosk by the beach for about a month when I started to notice little things. Clumps of seaweed spaced like footprints leading up to the edge of the sand in front of the kiosk. Seashells piled by the bench where I ate a sandwich before my shift. If I walked all the way down to the breakers, I'd find something washed up there, a diver's watch or a sports bottle or some other useful item.

At first I figured I was just lucky. It kept on happening, and only to me. When I asked the guys on the day shift if they'd noticed anything weird, Chuck and Dave gave me funny looks and laughed, telling me I was crazy. Maybe they were right.

The kiosk sat at one end of the lot, next to the exit lane. Tuesday night I chained my bike to the rack behind the kiosk then stepped inside and set my book bag on the shelf under the counter. On the back of the door was the bulletin board. A memo from my supervisor Roy was thumbtacked to it, reminding all of us to check the far corners of the lot. We'd had trouble in the past with bums sleeping over, kids necking, people doing drug deals. Lately I'd been avoiding those corners. They were closest to the beach, right where I'd find the seaweed tracks. Now I'd have to go all the way out there.

I turned my chair sideways and faced the cars. The radio and my textbooks would keep my imagination busy. Only a few people came in and out of the lot. Roy had warned me how slow it would be Monday through Thursday nights. That was all right with me. The shorter junior college summer schedule meant tests were already coming up.

When the fog rolled in it blurred the parking lines just enough to make the kiosk feel like an island about to be swallowed by the sea. At closing time I had to check the lot for any last cars and hang the chain across the entrance. That meant walking all the way out to

135

those corners. I felt a queasy flutter in my stomach as I stuffed the kiosk's flashlight in my jacket pocket and stepped outside.

The waves crashed against the beach. They sounded louder, closer. All that stood between them and me were a lot of empty parking spaces. The fog was so thick it stuck to my face like spiderwebs. The salt taste made my stomach churn. I settled for shining the flashlight's beam into the far corners, looking for the red gleam of taillights. I didn't see any, so I circled back around the kiosk to the entrance. I fastened the clasp at the end of the chain to the pole on the other side of the entrance, then started walking back toward the kiosk.

The chain rattled. I spun around. Through the misty columns of light thrown by the streetlights, a thin shadow floated toward me. A hand, long-fingered and bony, reached for me. I jumped back.

"Have I startled you? Forgive me." The hand was attached to an older man wearing a blue blazer over a gray sweater and slacks. His smile was friendly, but the angle of the streetlight hid his eyes. "I'm William Corbett. My friends call me Bill." He sounded like one of my professors. "I take it you're the new night man?"

"That's right." Bill's hand was still out. I shook it. "Jim Thompson."

"A lonely task this is, but fine if you like the sea."

"I don't."

"No? What a pity. May I ask why?"

I shrugged. If Chuck and Dave thought I was nuts, I'd better not tell anyone else. "I just--I feel like it's coming to get me. That's all."

"How sad. The sea is your friend. Your brain swims in it with every pulse of your blood."

That thought was so repulsive I clenched my eyes shut against it. Bill chuckled.

"I suspect you have a touch of thalassaphobia. That's the morbid fear of the sea."

"What do you know about it?"

"Quite a lot. You see, my wife was just the opposite. She loved the sea, and it loved her." Bill's voice hardened. "It loved her to death."

"Oh. Well. I have to go now." I backed toward the kiosk.

"Are you tired of being a slave to your fear? I can cure it."

That stopped me. "Are you serious?"

Bill pulled a gold card case out of his breast pocket, opened it and held out a business card. I took it. He had a string of letters after his name, the address of an office in the expensive part of town, and three phone numbers. I recognized one.

"You work at North Valley?"

"On a consulting basis." Bill smiled. "Students are referred to me when their difficulties fall under my specialty."

"What's that?"

"Anxieties and phobias. Rather a lucky coincidence that we met, yes?"

"I don't know. I mean, I can't really afford--"

"Please." Bill held up one hand. "Thalassaphobia is relatively rare. I'd welcome the opportunity to learn more about it."

"You really know something that will work?"

"We can certainly give it a try. Say tomorrow night, after your shift?"

"Okay."

"Until tomorrow, then." He walked off across the parking lot.

I stared after him. The clothes, the fancy card, all those degrees.... Bill had to be for real. Maybe I did have this phobia thing, but at least I wasn't crazy.

☙❧☙❧☙❧

My Wednesday shift crawled by. The stink of the sea reminded me of my old Biology text, making me think of the nasty little monsters that live in coral reefs. In the back of my mind I'd always thought something evil lurked down in the dark water, waiting for a chance to grab my ankles and drag me under. Its fishy lidless eyes watched me. Now I knew there was no monster. It was just this phobia thing.

By ten-thirty the lot was empty. I fastened the chain across the entrance and hurried back to the kiosk, keeping an eye on the blurry shadows. Bill was waiting by the door. He pulled a flask out of his jacket pocket and handed it to me.

"Take a good dose of that."

I took a sip. The Scotch burned a trail down my throat and warmed my stomach.

"Now," Bill said. "Let's get you out where we can do you some good."

He led me along the empty boardwalk and up the pier to the railing. Bill stared down at the water, then up at the stars.

"It's a marvelous world we live in, Jim. The more we make friends with it, the more it reveals its marvels to us."

"Some marvels I'd rather not see."

"You have to confront the fear before you can conquer it." He stared out at the water. "The sea waits to conquer you. Any slip, any carelessness, and it will strike."

"You mean--your wife?"

"We were out in the Caribbean, on a friend's yacht. Rosalind insisted on going for a swim." His breath hissed out between his teeth. "The seaweed trapped her. Before I could dive in and cut her free, it was too late."

"How awful." The weird look on his face made me nervous.

"The sea embraced her like a lover." He glared down at the waves. "A cold, merciless, demanding lover."

I backed off a step. That snapped him out of it.

"Let's get started. Close your eyes and listen to the water. Can you hear the breakers?"

I nodded.

"They crest, and break." His voice eased down to a deep whisper. "Crest, and break. Just like your breath. Feel the rhythm of your breath, Jim. Sink into it."

I listened. My breath slowed until it matched the sound of the waves. I still felt edgy, but more about Bill than the water.

"Listen to the tide, Jim. Listen to your heartbeat, pumping all that salt water through your veins." His voice rolled over me, heavy and soft. "Hear the gentle tide inside your body, and the gentle tide outside it too. All the same, Jim. All the same. Your heart and the sea's, beating together."

I listened, feeling calmer.

"The sea is your friend, Jim. You do want to be friends with the sea, don't you? You want to be happy and calm, like you are right now."

"Yes..."

"Reach out to the sea, Jim. Show it you want to be friends."

My right hand moved a little. I thought of Bill's wife trapped in the seaweed, and those seaweed tracks outside the kiosk. I tensed up again.

"I can't."

"Tell me why, Jim. Why does the sea frighten you?"

The answer came out before I could stop it. "I keep finding things. Little stuff, just shells and tracks in the sand and little presents. I thought maybe they were for somebody else, but it just keeps happening. I mean, am I paranoid or what?"

"Not at all." He didn't say anything for a minute. "That's how it always starts. The sea gives, but it always wants to be paid back."

Before I could ask him what he meant, he pushed me closer to the rail.

"I suspect your fear of the sea might be just a symptom of something deeper. Think, now. Think back to when you were a little boy."

His voice weighed me down again, sending me back through memories. I remembered salt stinging my eyes and a bad taste in my mouth as I threw up. Then it all came back. I was six, at the beach. My father hoisted me up over his head and carried me way out into the waves. We were both laughing. Then he threw me in. I kept fighting my way to the surface, screaming for help. Dad just stood there and yelled at me to swim. Finally, my sister swam out and carried me back to shore. Old shame and anger flooded me, hot and ugly. I shoved away from the rail. Bill's hands on my shoulders kept me there.

"I'm right here, Jim. Everything is fine. Tell me what you're thinking."

"My father--he thought it was so funny. He threw me in and left me there." Tears welled up, choking off my voice. "I was screaming, thrashing around. He just stood there laughing."

"I see. Could it be, Jim, that your real problem is your rage at your father? You're really afraid of what might happen if you turned that rage loose."

I stopped straining backward. That made sense. My sister and I weren't allowed to get angry at Dad, could never show any sign of it. I started to cry harder, feeling stupid and awful and better all at once. Bill patted me on the back.

"You've achieved quite a breakthrough. All that's left now is to replace your old fear of the sea with good associations. When I tell you it's all right now, you'll have no fear of the sea at all. Understand?" I nodded. "Wake up now."

Bill snapped his fingers right in front of my face. I jerked back. My eyes opened.

"There now," he said. "Have a look at the water and tell me how you feel."

I glanced at the water, shrugged. "No problem."

"Excellent. Shall we try again tomorrow night? We'll have an opportunity we must not miss."

"An opportunity for what?" There was something about his smile, a manic eagerness, I didn't like.

"The moon will be full. The power of its light will chase the darkness out of the water and cure your fear."

That didn't sound like anything I'd read in my Psych texts. "Sounds more like magic than psychology."

He gave me an odd look, then laughed. "There's a little of both in each."

Something still bothered me. "I can see how Dad being a jerk started all this, but what about the stuff I keep finding?"

Bill waved that away. "It's probably nothing more than a mild delusion. You wish your father would apologize, perhaps by giving you toys. Since you can't confront him directly, you've transferred that wish to the sea itself."

That made a strange kind of sense. "Look, I'd really like to thank you for your help. Can I buy you dinner or something?"

He shook his head, smiling that same disturbing smile. "Tomorrow night will settle a number of debts."

The next night after closing I met Bill at the end of the pier. Over his sweater and slacks he wore a poncho of black silk. Seagull feathers, fish bones, chipped seashells and bits of colored glass decorated it. As I got closer I could see silvery symbols embroidered onto the cloth. He had on a necklace of cowrie shells. A flat circle of mother-of-pearl hung off it. More symbols were scratched onto that.

"Hey, Bill," I said. "What's all that for?"

"The Orb of Dreams and the Sphere of Conquest stand side by

side in the heavens, with Venus suspended between them. On such a night can miracles occur."

"What are you talking about?"

He blinked at me, then chuckled. "Psychodrama. Shamans have been curing people with it for thousands of years."

He made it sound perfectly natural, but something about that get-up bothered me. He'd put a lot of time into it, so he couldn't have made it just for me.

"First, a toast for luck." He handed me his flask. I took a swig. The Scotch had a peculiar gritty edge to it. He probably got sand in the cap. I handed it back.

"Now watch the water," he said. "See how it swirls. Follow it, around and around. Sink into the rhythm of the water. Feel it in your breath, in your blood."

The Scotch filled me with its bracing fire. The heat moved out of my stomach and along my arms and legs, up into my head. My tongue felt thick. My eyes swung back and forth with the current. The swirl of the water wobbled and blurred.

He pulled me away from the rail and made me sit on the bench near the stairway that led down to the fishing platforms below the pier.

"Stay right here." He hurried down the stairs.

Something was very wrong. I tried to stand up. None of my muscles even twitched. Hypnotism was supposed to make you suggestible, but not turn you into a robot. What had the old man done to me? The scotch. It had to be whatever made the scotch taste funny.

"Please." Bill's voice came from right below me. "I've waited so long. The stars, the tide, everything is in place."

The waves hit the pilings. I heard a hiss like steam shooting out of a bad radiator.

"Haven't I served you?" Bill asked. "You've taken everything, my youth, my love, my life itself!"

A slow hiss answered him.

"You thought you'd trap him with your petty trinkets, didn't you? You'll have him, all right, but only if you give me what you promised!" He hurried up the stairs and put a hand on my shoulder. "Come along, Jim. It's all right now."

I felt no fear of the water, but I was terrified of him. Even so, my body stood up and followed him. I felt like an engineer trapped inside a runaway train. I took one step after another down to the slimy, barnacle-crusted platform. It rocked a little with the strength of the rising tide. Bill grabbed a fistful of my jacket and jerked me right up to the platform's edge.

"Come here, Jim. Look at the water. Let it see you."

The water down here was dark, dark enough to smother the moonlight, dark enough to make every one of my coral reef nightmares come alive. My heart nearly pounded a hole right through my ribs. I begged my frozen muscles to run.

"Luna and Venus link arms in the heavens," Bill chanted. "Lovers return from graves long filled. The gates of death swing wide on hinges oiled by blood your priests have spilled!"

A larger wave sloshed onto the platform. Little wavelets ran toward my shoes. Nodding, Bill cackled. He made a paler shadow against the dark water. The bits of glass on his poncho glittered at me like lidless eyes. Those fishy lidless eyes... Raw panic exploded inside me. Straining as hard as I could, I dragged one foot back from the edge.

Bill stared at the water, looking confused, then furious. "Here he is, just as I promised. Now give me Rosalind!"

The water did nothing but stroke the toes of my sneakers. Bill growled and thrust a hand under his poncho. He pulled out a fishing knife and reached for me. The waves heaved beneath the platform. My one moving foot skidded in the slime and I fell over. Bill staggered backward, teetering on the platform's edge. A wall of dark water rose up behind him. I stared at it, praying it was only the drug in the scotch making me see things. Anything else meant this was real. The dark water crashed down over Bill. For a second I saw him trapped inside it, slashing at the water with the knife. Then it sank. I dragged myself to the edge of the platform and watched Bill disappear into the gloom. He fought all the way down.

I rolled over and sprawled on my back, still sluggish. The panic screamed at me to get away before the water grabbed me too. I tried to sit up. A stronger wave splashed across the platform. Something rattled. It was Bill's cowrie shell necklace. Another present, from the sea.

The waves lifted the platform again, gentler this time, like they were rocking me. I touched the necklace with a cautious fingertip.

The sea had never hurt me. That was just my father being a jerk. The dark water had saved my life. I sat up and dropped the necklace down over my head. The mother-of-pearl circle gleamed. My heartbeat slowed, beating in time with the waves that kissed the pilings and drew back like shy lovers.

The sea was my friend.

Juliet Silver and the Seeker of the Depths

by Wendy Nikel

Juliet Silver raised the doorknocker—a gilded image of a tentacled monster—and let it fall, sending a metallic *clang* up and down the deserted city street. Sunlight streamed over her, peeking out from the horizon with golden tendrils that seemed to tap her on the shoulder, to question what she was doing on the ground when the skies were so crisp and clear, so perfect for sailing.

As she waited, Juliet's fingers twitched at the hilt of her sword. It'd been months since she'd seen the sunrise from land, and she ached to rise above the dingy scraps of garbage and the hungry rats of the city's alleys. But Stenson, a rival captain of the airship *The Bearer of Bad News*, was insistent that she meet him today, this morning, at this particular shop.

Whatever the old codger wanted, it had better be worth her time.

When the bolt finally slid across, the iron door opened with a groan of its massive hinges. The door was large enough for a steam carriage to power through, and likely many did over the course of a week. Upon entering, however, Juliet's attention was drawn not to the carriages, nor even to the new-fangled bits and baskets, snares and rudders that she might have used to upgrade her own ship, *The Realm of Impossibility*.

Instead, she was drawn to an item sitting solidly in the center of the workshop, stout and bulbous and crouching like a frog. Its outer shell gleamed so that within its curves and panels, her reflection stared back at her. The metal was cold to her touch.

"Meets your approval, captain?"

Juliet caught Stenson's reflection as he stepped beside her. She didn't turn but proceeded to walk about the contraption, examining every inch of it.

"For exploring underseas, I take it?" She knocked upon its side. "I have to wonder how well it would hold up to the water pressure."

"Just as well as it's sitting here before you. The iron-welder who built it is one of the city's finest."

"I'd much like to meet him."

"He's a solitary type. Doesn't care much for pleasantries or small talk."

Curious that he would make Stenson's acquaintance then. The old man was quite the gossipmonger. Juliet wisely kept this opinion to herself.

"And the headlights?" She cast a skeptical glace at the blue domed lights. They hardly looked as though they'd cut through fog, much less a murky sea.

"Mostly for show. This craft has something even better, Miss Silver." The older captain reached forward and sprung the door open. Its pneumatic hinges hissed. Inside, a flat screen blinked to life. "Sonar. Even if the windows are filled with grime, you'll be able to see any obstacles before you as clear as a pretty spring day."

"And what do you intend to do with this little fish?"

"I intend to give her to you."

Ah, now the real bargaining would begin. Stenson wasn't the generous type; Juliet wondered what the real price would be. "And what do you want from me?"

"I want the treasure of the *Argonaut* — the largest haul of stolen gold and gems anyone has ever seen, lost beneath the Sea of Prosperity. And I want you to fetch it for me."

"I'm not a dog." Juliet brushed past him, making her way for the door.

"No, you're not. You're a shrewd captain, one who's daring enough to go where none has before."

Juliet hesitated, her hand upon the door. Well, he wasn't *wrong*.

"And wise enough to know that this little fish—" Stenson said, tapping the hull of the underwater vehicle "—could make you rich beyond your dreams. We both know that the *Argonaut* wasn't the first airship to plummet from the sky into troubled waves, though its treasure is the only one I wish to stake a claim upon. After delivering it to me and receiving your share—"

"Sixty percent."

"Thirty, and don't interrupt. After receiving your share, this little *Seeker of the Depths* will be yours to do with as you wish. It won't take a daring young lass such as yourself to make a fine fortune in underwater salvaging. I'd do it myself if I were a few decades younger."

Juliet considered this as she resumed her perusal of the machine. The interior was small, intended only for one diver. The rest of her crew would have to wait above the surface; she didn't trust anyone else to the task. She'd be lying if she said that the coffers of wealth in the belly of the *Argonaut* didn't tempt her.

"Are you daring enough?"

It was Stenson's voice that spoke aloud, an echo of the question already swirling about her heart and mind. A question to which she already knew the answer.

"Yes."

☠☠☠

The *Seeker* was strapped to the *Realm of Impossibility* with great lengths of chain that clanked and rattled like bones. All along the dock, crews neglected their own ships to watch the activity about Juliet's. She stood before the gangplank, arms crossed over her chest and feet planted, daring them with her scowl to come forth and stake their claim. The *Argonaut*'s treasure was, after all, pirate's booty, and there were plenty among the airpilots who'd fallen victim to it.

Geoffries, her first mate, was the only one who approached. "You know they won't raise arms against you today. They'll wait until you've returned with the prize… if you return at all."

"Do you doubt me, Geoffries?"

"Not I, Captain. But they don't know you as I do. Undoubtedly most expect that your little bronze fish will sink to the depths with you in its belly and neither of you will be seen again."

"Fools."

"The ship's prepared, Captain," a crewmember called out.

Juliet took a final, defiant glance about her and—with firm footfalls upon the grated gangplank—took her place on the *Realm of Impossibility.*

☠☠☠

The Sea of Prosperity was a misnomer at best — a putrid soup of grease at worst. Even the skies above it were a swamp of foul-smelling brown. Not a single bird traversed the clouds, and neither did Juliet expect to find anything living beneath the water's stagnant surface.

Geoffries looked on as Juliet strapped herself into the *Seeker*'s chamber. It was some sort of recklessness, perhaps, that would lead a woman to crawl into that round, iron coffin and allow herself to be lowered into the sea. But she'd tested the equipment herself, and if all went well, she'd return in just a few hours. In the meantime, she'd simply crawl along the seabed, picking through who-knows-what-she'd-find-there until she uncovered the wreckage of the *Argonaut* and the treasure hidden within it.

"All set, Captain?"

"Aye, aye!"

The door hissed shut and sealed, leaving Juliet in such an absolute silence that — had it not been for the movement seen through the window — she'd have thought the outside world had ceased to exist. With an abrupt, jarring motion and the faraway clanking of iron chains, the *Seeker of the Depths* descended.

Murky water closed over the window. Glistening particles floated in the rays of sun that somehow cut through the layers of silt and sediment. These bright specks of light grew sparser as the vessel descended and the darkness deepened. Finally, the *Seeker* settled on the ocean floor. Outside the window, all was black and still, save for the occasional flick of a phosphorescent tail fin.

Juliet flicked on the sonar. She pulled handles and turned levers to operate the vessel's spidery legs, dragging it meter by meter across the sea floor. The sonar flickered with outlines of flat expanses, jagged cliffs, and crevices that seemed to descend into the center of the earth.

Juliet had hardly begun her search when the *Seeker* became stuck. She wrenched at levers and pressed dials, but though the iron mechanisms rattled, the *Seeker* refused to move. Cursing Stenson, Juliet pressed the distress signal.

148

She sat in the never-changing stillness of the depths, waiting for the chattering of the chain and the lightening of the murk that would indicate the *Realm of Impossibility* was lifting her to the surface, but it never came. Was she too deep for the *Realm* to receive her signal? Had the chain broken somehow? Juliet was just debating her next course of action when the *Seeker* jerked into motion.

She fumbled with the controls. The vessel was moving, but the comforting rattle of its spider legs was missing. Had some sea creature had swooped in and gobbled her up? Considering the blackness around her, it seemed possible. Except... the sonar still showed the landscape of the deeps.

Had something crept up and snagged her from behind? If so, there was little she could do about it now, besides to be ready when it stopped. She gripped her knife and studied the sonar.

Finally, the *Seeker* reached a cliff wall. Instead of going around it, however, the vessel proceeded through what appeared to be a narrow tunnel. It opened out into a vast cavern — a cavern filled with light.

Juliet blinked against the sudden brilliance. The cavern ceiling arched high overhead, glowing with light from thousands, millions, perhaps billions of phosphorescent creatures swimming about. Some were the size of whales, while others were so small that their lights seemed like those of fireflies buzzing about.

Beneath this sea of magnificent creatures was an even more magnificent sight — a city, constructed of glass panes, crisscrossed and held up by frames of shining gold. As the *Seeker* drew nearer, Juliet could see the people wandering about inside, people with golden skin coming out of golden houses and walking down golden roads, conversing and carrying on about their lives as if nothing was more natural than living leagues beneath the surface.

A panel opened in the side of the city, and the *Seeker* was carried inside a narrow tunnel — an airlock, in fact — where all the water rushed out around it. Juliet pressed the release button on her craft and jumped out, wielding her knife.

The *Seeker* had, indeed, been captured from behind by a craft not too unlike it. They shared the same bulbous shape and the same thin, spidery legs, but this one also had front appendages that now held the *Seeker* in place.

"Stenson," Juliet seethed. He must have known about this

place, about these people and their craft. How else could his design be so strikingly similar? Had he stolen their ship, or merely the design? Her breath came hot and furious, but she didn't fight as two armed guards grabbed her from behind.

The hatch of the larger craft sprung open and a man with golden skin and close-cropped hair leaned out. "Take her to the Queen."

"Yes," Juliet said between clenched teeth. "I'd very much like to speak with her."

⚜ ⚜ ⚜

None of the other structures came near the opulence of the palace's shimmering walls. Every inch of it was composed of pearls stacked into bricks, each one perfectly polished and luminescent. Its sprawling courtyard contained innumerous metal sculptures of all types of sea life. These creatures ran by clockwork, rattling and chattering as they stretched and dove and swam through the air.

As the guards led Juliet through the entrance, she took note of the squid whose head made up the capstone and whose tentacles cascaded down either side of the doorway, a skillful piece of metalwork. From there, they entered a cavernous throne room. At the far end, separated by a carpet of tiny, polished shells, sat the Queen. She wore a sparkling robe of fish scales and a crown composed of dozens of tiny fish ribs that rose in intricate whorls to a peak high above her brow. Her face was long and golden and unlined, though her eyes looked old and wise. She was flanked on either side by a pair of ladies in lavish gowns and bright, bejeweled headdresses.

Juliet shook free from the guards' grasp and dipped her head in a reverent bow.

"What have you brought me?" The Queen's voice was clear and crisp as glass, though in it, also, was the sharp edge of the same.

"Please, your majesty," Juliet said before the guards could speak. "I am Juliet Silver, captain of the airship *The Realm of Impossibility*, explorer of the skies."

"What purpose would an airship captain have in the dominion of the water-dwellers? Surely you know of the truce and punishment due to those who break it."

150

Juliet seethed silently at Stenson. "I knew of no such truce, nor—truly—of your glorious city's existence."

"How is it possible you've never heard of the great and powerful city of Prosperia? Has it been so long since we closed our gates that all have forgotten our existence?"

Juliet stood silently. Certainly, she'd heard of the undersea city of Prosperia, but it was a myth, a legend, a bedtime story to amuse small children. To find that it was true was akin to discovering the mythical Bandybell's lair.

"Liska." The Queen turned to one of her ladies-in-waiting. "How many years have passed since our isolation?"

"Five hundred twenty-two, your Highness."

"Hardly a bat of the eye... yet perhaps for you short-lived folk with your warring and wandering that would be long enough to forget. Still, I find it hard to believe this warning would not have been passed down from the older, more experienced captains to the younger ones."

"Indeed." It would certainly explain why Stenson — superstitious man that he was — had no desire to dive beneath the waves himself. He'd certainly have heard the stories, though Juliet — a newcomer to the skies and without a mentor to guide her — had not. Had he hoped Juliet might slip past the Propserians and recover the *Argonaut*'s treasure? Or was this all a ruse to get rid of her? "Well, now that we've established my innocence, if you could return me to my vessel—"

"My dear girl." The Queen rose to her feet and cast her deep shadow upon Juliet. "Ignorance is not akin to innocence. In order to preserve our isolation, we are quite unable to allow your return."

"I see." Juliet narrowed her eyes. "And what is my punishment to be?"

"It just so happens that this is a year of sacrifice to the kraken. I trust you'll make him a fine morsel at festival time. Until then..." She turned to one of the ladies on her right. "Sofia, please bind her. Then the guards shall take her to her cell."

The lady she spoke to rose, dipped her hand in a pocket, and pulled out a length of delicate chain. She bound Juliet's hands with nimble fingers and from another pocket procured a tiny lock, with which she secured the restraints. She pulled upon them to test their strength and — as she did so — a small sliver of metal dropped into

Juliet's palms.

Any thought that this slip might have been inadvertent left Juliet's mind when the woman met her eyes. Then she turned and announced to the Queen, "The prisoner is bound."

The Queen nodded, and with that, the guards led Juliet away.

⁂

The cell beneath the ocean floor was spongy and smelled of rotting fish. Juliet stood in the dark, turning over in her hands the tiny lock pick — for that's what the lady Sofia had slipped to her — as she waited. For what, she wasn't certain. On the surface, it'd have been for the darkest part of night, but here the hours stretched on without a single variance of the phosphorescent glow that bled in streaks through the grated window high above her, nor to the pacing of the guard beyond her door.

She'd just resigned herself to try to get a small bit of sleep when the sound of a commotion in the hall outside her door sent a rush of adrenaline through her, dulling any thought of slumber.

Immediately, she set out to pick the lock on the door. Gears within it turned and the bolt retracted. The corridor beyond was empty, save for a slim figure in a long gown, heels, and a massive, jeweled headdress, carrying a small jar with one of the phosphorescent creatures swimming about in it.

Lady Sofia.

"Quickly!" Sofia said. "The guard will return any moment."

Juliet followed her through winding pathways, their feet squishing on the soggy dungeon floor. When the lady paused in a quiet corner to catch her breath, Juliet's tongue loosened.

"Who are you? And why are you helping me?"

"Sofia... the royal tinker. And I'm not helping you; you're helping me... to escape."

"Escape? Why?"

"You think we enjoy being trapped down here with no contact to the outside world? Our isolation was based on the Queen's own emotional pride alone, not any logical rationale. She only cut us off to punish him for leaving." She set off again down the dark corridor, and Juliet followed on her heels.

"Who? Who left?"

"Her son, the heir. When her search for him proved futile, she flew into a rage and commanded Prosperia be cut off from the world above. Now hush, or someone will hear."

"Do you have a weapon?" Juliet whispered. Without her sword or knife, she felt positively helpless, completely at the mercy of this overdressed aristocrat. Sofia reached up to her headdress and pulled out a hat pin the length of her hand and passed it to Juliet, who took it with some skepticism. It was no dagger, for certain, but it was better than nothing.

They turned a corner and Sofia screeched, nearly backing up directly into Juliet. The guard had returned by another route and was blocking their path, his sword at the ready.

Juliet stepped in front of Sofia, brandishing the hairpin. The guard smirked, obviously unimpressed. Juliet lunged. With a quick, well-placed jab, she pierced the gap between his chest plate and helmet, causing him to cry out and giving her the element of surprise needed to knock his sword from his hand. Finally, a proper weapon!

"Lie down on the ground," she instructed him, "and count to three hundred. If we meet again, I will not be so merciful."

Juliet urged Sofia on, and the bewildered woman took off down the corridor once again. Juliet paused now and again to glance behind her and see that the guard was still lying prone, as Sofia rushed further ahead. She climbed a flight of stairs, and Juliet rushed to follow, blinking as her eyes adjusted to the brilliance of the phosphorescent light.

At the top of the steps, Juliet stopped short.

Sofia stood before her with a guard's blade pressed to her throat. On either side of her stood a dozen other guards, their swords drawn. Juliet hesitated, her mind racing to devise a strategy that would leave Sofia unharmed. She was just about to step forward when the guards shifted, parting in the center to admit the Queen herself.

"I see that I've a traitor in my midst. Dear Sofia... I do hope the kraken doesn't mind if his feast begins early; I could hardly hope to keep you contained in the locks and chains you designed yourself."

"If you lay a hand on her..." Juliet began, holding her weapon steady.

The Queen raised her eyebrows and placed a hand upon her

chin, as if amused. On the third finger, she bore a dark ring with a design Juliet recognized from the palace's curved arch — the kraken. "Go on. What shall you do?"

Juliet lowered her sword, her eyes transfixed on the ring. The palace entrance wasn't the first place she'd seen that design.

"You will allow Sofia and me to return to the surface unhindered, and I, in turn, will tell you where to find your son."

⁂ ⁂ ⁂

Juliet stood on the deserted city street once again and raised the ten-legged doorknocker — the gilded kraken. Beside her stood two women, dressed in long cloaks and hoods to protect their golden skin from the rays of the early morning sun.

The *Realm of Impossibility*'s crew had been surprised at Juliet's return after they believed they'd lost her, and even more surprised at the two strange women she'd brought with her. Juliet had held off on answering their questions, promising she'd explain all once she'd held up her deal of the bargain.

The bolt slid across and the door opened with a *creak*. This time, it was not Stenson who opened it, but a lean man donned in a smock, long gloves, and an iron-welder's mask over his face. Upon seeing the three in the doorway, the iron-welder slowly raised his mask, exposing his golden skin.

"Mother?"

The Queen rushed forward to embrace him. Juliet and Sofia hung back, though Juliet could see how the tinkerer's eyes danced about the workroom, taking in all the tools and metalwork there. The *Realm*, too, had fascinated the Queen's lady-in-waiting, and Juliet had spent much of their journey back to the city explaining the airship's inner workings to her.

"Let's leave them to their reunion," she whispered to Sofia.

They waited beside the iron door, watching the carriages bustling past and people walking to the market as the city awakened to a new day.

"I'm sorry you lost your vessel," Sofia said.

"It wasn't mine. Not yet anyway."

"Will its owner hold you accountable for its loss, then?"

"Perhaps." If Stenson wanted the *Seeker* back, he'd have to

154

retrieve it from the Queen himself. As for the *Argonaut* and its treasure, when Juliet had questioned her earlier, Sofia verified that the wreck had already been picked apart by Prosperian scavengers. They'd used every bit of metal for repairs of their underwater city.

"What are your plans now, as a free woman?" Juliet asked, breaking the silence.

"I... I don't know." Sofia fiddled with the buttons and levers on her belt. The metal jangled like a song and glimmered in the sun. "I hadn't dared to hope for anything beyond escape."

"I've a proposition for you, then." Juliet spied an airship on the horizon and shielded her eyes against the sun. "The *Realm of Impossibility* could use a good tinkerer on board, someone to help out when the mechanical parts require repairs. Tell me, how do you feel about the skies?"

Sofia looked up from her belt, startled. Then, she, too, raised her eyes to the blue sky and slowly, a smile spread across her golden face.

FOR EACH OF THESE

MISERIES

by Premee Mohamed

The fortress appeared as a distant dot in the submersible's foot-thick window, the first thing Gene had seen for hours not illuminated by the headlight. Terrible things had swum in front of the powerful beam — curious, startled, returning for second looks, sometimes carrying a little light of their own. Too many legs, too much mouth, not enough body, till her nerves were shot and she folded against the sub's wall. The Foundation ship had dropped her like a penny into a fountain — make a wish! — and vanished into tropical warmth.

"Hear that?" the pilot whispered as he cut tether, muffled by the roar of the bubbles. "That's your heart beating, doctor. The sound reflecting back. That's the quiet down there."

He hadn't deserved a response; but he was right, and Gene had sunk in silence except for the drumming of her pulse as it bounced from the curved titanium walls. She squeezed back into the window seat, hoping the dot was closer. It wasn't, but the rectilinear forms she'd glimpsed earlier were clearer. Old volcanic formations, like the Giant's Causeway she'd visited in Ireland? These lacked the giant's crisp workmanship and had blurred from ancient seismic events and the gentle, endless fall of marine snow — plankton, bones, scales, seaweed, plastic, excrement, teeth, larvae. Its pockets of darkness remained so as the headlight passed, not even tubeworms fleeing the beam. Strange.

She woke as the autopilot docked against the fort's airlock. Her ears had become so sensitized that she could hear the soldiers outside — guttural grunts and whispered directions. "Here... uh.... Left. Up. One...two...three!"

The door was pulled to by a half-dozen young men. Gene breathed deep of the real air — armpits, iodine, mold. And things she couldn't recognize, as often happened in or on the ocean, things that a land dweller's olfactory library lacked.

"This way," the lead soldier said, not bothering with the usual introductions; he looked grimly irritated. That was odd, Gene thought. Folks stationed underwater usually loved anything that broke up the monotony. She hefted her duffel bag and splashed after him.

⁂

General Rotherford looked just like he did in her mother's photos, Gene thought as she shook his big, cold hand.

"Doctor...Borometz," he said.

She waited another beat for him to recognize either her face or the name, then said, "Yes, General. I'm Ephigenia Borometz's daughter."

As she had hoped, his expression of pouched worry dawned into not quite happiness but relief, a slow recognition of the progeny of someone he used to like and trust, and by extrapolation perhaps also likeable, also trustworthy.

"I didn't know you were in charge down here, sir," she said. "I thought you had retired by now. I mean, only because Mom is about to — " she added, hoping he wouldn't be insulted.

"I would, if they'd let me," Rotherford chuckled. "Still a 'valued member.' How is Effie these days?"

"Good. Still on the platform."

"Doin' reservoir stuff, I suppose," the general murmured; their silence became an awkward reverie. Gene knew the story. Theo Rotherford and Effie Borometz had been the star team of their professor's research ship, until the war began, and they'd been drafted into the deep-stealth submersible program. After the armistice, Effie veered into reservoir hydrogeology and Rotherford stuck with their abyssal beasts. When they met for lunch two years later, Effie was making triple his salary, and had a partner and a toddler. They had swapped Christmas cards for a while, but the former best friends would never be the same. Here, perhaps, was a chance to mend some bridges.

"The Foundation didn't brief me much," Gene said. "I mean, I was lying in bed watching Netflix about sixteen hours ago, sir. Can you tell me why I'm here?"

He gestured at one of the other soldiers. "Not so's you won't laugh at a crazy old man," he said. "Corporal?"

The corporal, a middle-aged guy, handsome in that swaggering way that might have looked nice on a recruiting poster if it were less creased and folded with anxiety, flinched. "I mean," the man said, "for starters, we requested a squad of sixty, fully armed. And we got you. So, the men are already pissed off with the Foundation."

"With me, you mean," Gene said.

He shrugged. "Can you blame them? They get a lady, a kid really. A *scientist*. When we wanted men and firepower."

"Maybe your problem can't be solved with firepower," she said. "Which I'd be able to assess if you told me about it. Right?"

Janz glanced at the other soldier, a short, tired-looking woman in a baggy regulation uniform, and at their signal, Gene followed them into the maze of corridors.

"Been down here before?" the woman said.

Gene glanced at the stitched nametag: Dr. Ruiz. Ah, a scientist — that explained her presence in the office. The base boasted a rotating crew of a few dozen scientists, using it as both lab and field base.

"No. They didn't even tell me the name. Just kept calling it the Raj."

Ruiz laughed. "That's rich. Makes it sound like some kinda luxury resort." She pointed as she walked, both of them trotting to keep up with the corporal. "Well, welcome to the High-Pressure Eastern Ostermann-Rajatnaram Oceanic Tower. We mostly just call it the ROT because everything's kind of falling apart and fungusy. Visitors are always like 'Why didn't they call it MASH or something' but the letters didn't work out... Anyway, we're in the west wing — that way's north. Try to keep your bearings or you'll get lost and have to sleep in a broom closet. We've all done it. That's the west Canteen, they call that Oscar's. That's Warehouse One, Warehouse Two, Warehouse Five. We're not real good at numbering here. That's the autoclave room. That's Sample Processing One."

Gene let the names wash over her, trusting some part of her

backbrain to record it as they walked. The fortress was her age almost to the day, built, like her, midway through the war; but it was visibly disintegrating in a way that was not merely frightening given how much water waited outside to crush and suffocate them, but surprising given the work she knew had gone into its design. Indeed, some of that work had been by her mother and General Rotherford. It wasn't being maintained, that was it. A lack of manpower? Her dossier had said there had been recent fatalities as well as damage to the facility, but not how, or even when. It had been frighteningly vague for a quasi-military document.

"We're here," the corporal said. Gene caught her breath as the dining room's automatic doors swished open, a brief wash of ammonia-stinking water lapping at their rubber boots. For a moment she thought she could hear her heart again. But it was just the syncopated swishing of a mopping robot running prissily over the walls and floors, hubcap-sized but tiny in the dripping chaos of the room.

"What happened here?"

"That's what we need you to figure out," he muttered. "Something...attacked last week. Smashed some of the windows. The shutters and doors reacted just like they were s'posed to. Sealed shut. Twelve casualties — not all drowned. Five missing after we pumped all the water out."

"But..." She grabbed at the wall, her boots sliding on the glossy black-and-white tile. "Missing? Attacked from the *outside*? I don't understand how..."

He continued quietly, as if the mention of the attacks might bring on another one. Speak of the devil and he shall appear, Gene thought. Five in six months — nothing that had gotten inside, not till the dining room, but the supply sub hangars had been destroyed, cutting the fort off from its own transportation; ladders had been torn away from the main structure, a few outbuildings smashed, their sides dramatically caved in despite everything they had been built to withstand. As if something huge and malevolent but not terribly intelligent or methodical had discovered this thing in its territory and sought to evict the intruder.

"So, we wanted to find out what's doin' it," the corporal said as they stopped outside Central Research. "And Dr. Wong here sez there's nothing down here that could. So that's why you got called, I guess. Because maybe she doesn't know all the things in this area. Because there's things, and then there's...*things*."

"But you do weapons testing here," Gene ventured. "You're a fueling stop for NATO subs, an intelligence hotspot. It could be..."

"We know when a bogey's coming from hours away," he snapped. "It ain't enemy hostiles, if that's what you're suggesting."

"Occam's Razor," she said. "This fortress was designed by humans, and only humans could breach the defenses. It's crazy to think some deep-sea creature... I mean, not even a *whale*, not that you get them at this depth. Not a shark, not a squid, not a manta ray. Nothing is big and heavy enough to get through that glass, or fast enough. There's nothing."

"Look at the bodies and tell me one more time that it's nothing," he said.

But after a cursory examination under Dr. Wong's anxious, hopeful supervision — virtually all Gene knew of human anatomy was the effects of water pressure — she could only guess that projectile window shards, or perhaps being pulled against the broken frames, had killed these men...if they hadn't killed each other.

Gene looked uneasily at the glowering corporal, who had finally introduced himself as Fergus Janz. Maybe they had experienced some kind of... deep-sea psychosis, brains bubbling with malevolent gases, hallucinogenic neurotransmitters... but it seemed wrong, off somehow. Nothing made of man seemed to belong here. The corpses even smelled wrong, not the ordinary sad reek of a semi-thawed human body but a virulent green-black stench, nothing she knew, not rotten seaweed, not blood, not mold.

☙❧☙❧☙❧

Retrieving her bag from Rotherford's office, Gene was peremptorily informed that a welcome party had been scheduled in the East dining room, and word was spreading that she'd come to fix everything.

"Everything, General," Gene said. "Come on."

"I didn't start that rumor," Rotherford said in the same tone. "What I been telling people is closer to the truth. That you came down to assess and evaluate. And after you make your report, we'll get the men and the firepower. It's your word they need, that's all.

They won't believe us. They think we're cracked, you know. Pelagic fever or brain bubbles or whathaveyou. They won't listen."

Gene looked away, ashamed. There was a gleam in the old man's eye that she had initially thought could be, yes, some kind of chemical imbalance. They all had a little of it — Janz, Wong, Ruiz, even the young soldiers at the dock. But whatever Rotherford had was so pronounced it reminded her of Victorian descriptions of a laudanum high, his pupils wide, lit from the inside. Had that been there in the old photos? "East wing," she said eventually. "I'll be there. I won't have to give a speech, will I?"

"No promises," he chuckled.

"I'm going to take my sub out," she said. "I've got hours to kill. Maybe I'll see...clues, evidence, something."

"Sure. What's that seat, three?" he said; she blinked, taken aback by his agreement. "Take Ruiz and one more scientist. And tether up."

⁂

The sound of three hearts beating evened out to a dull, comforting thrum, substituting an artificial engine noise for the sub's silent mini-nuke propulsion drive. The ground was too far below them to be seen, but Gene knew it would be flat, soft, snow-white. Just like the stuff that had turned the basalt formations into cotton candy. The hunt for clues was a joke; the black water was featureless. She thought of the scientific illustration classes she'd taken in grad school, knocking a bottle of India ink over once with her dip pen, the blackness flooding across the page, buckling it into a contorted bestiary, vanishing the animals already drawn.

"I've never seen anything out here," Ruiz said, looking at the wall monitor, a magnified version of the image visible through the tiny porthole. "But we don't do much recon. Just for tests."

"I've seen squid and anglerfish," said the scientist they'd borrowed, Atwood. "I thought I saw an oarfish once. We're not in a dead zone."

Gene steered the little sub towards the lava formations, bracing herself as the light spilled across the dark crannies for whatever was in there to come shooting out. But just as before, nothing did, not a single fish, not one shrimp or jelly or worm. As

162

she circled the formations their heartbeats grew louder and louder, till she could almost feel the vibration under her fingertips.

"Have these been thoroughly checked out?" she said, her voice distant to her ears.

"Yeah," Ruiz said. "The General went out himself. Nothing."

"They look like skyscrapers, don't they," Atwood said softly, and it was the visual equivalent of popping out an earplug — they *were* buildings, she realized. They weren't natural formations at all. The arches were carved, not merely curved; the openings were the lintels of windows and doors; the sparkle was not mica or quartz but glass and gold. And the random swirls of algae and detritus on the ruins weren't random; they had settled into the grooves of chiseled tableaux, made who knew how long ago.

"They've explored more of the moon, by percentage of area, than the deep ocean," Gene said after a minute. "And nothing on land's unknown now, with all that drone and satellite footage..."

"What are you saying?" Ruiz whispered.

The tether pulled taut, gently, as it was designed to do; the control panel beeped in warning. Time to return. It was getting too damp and hot anyway. Gene spun the sub to starboard and chewed on her lip. I'm from the mountains, she thought. The mountains, the *mountains*. My home is as far from the ocean, as far from this crushing darkness as you can get. Far from this thing that would kill us not even hatefully but all unknowing, blinking out our small pitiful light in its endless depth, as you might not even notice if you walked past a candle and the breath of your passing extinguished its flame. I do not belong here. And the ocean knows it.

Back at the dining room, escorted by a gangling young soldier with an Adam's apple as big as a Granny Smith, Gene helped General Rotherford set up for the party — juice and liquor, nothing carbonated; reconstituted pasta from the fort's long-suffering galley; bowls of stale chips, heaps of jerky and pepperoni; vases of pink flowers from the greenhouse, papery bougainvillea. The lights were acting up, giving her a headache — some high, keening whine coming from everywhere and nowhere. Rotherford could hear it too and kept twiddling the light switches as if it might help.

The room filled quickly, as any scientific or military gathering tended to, or at least anything with a lot of young people who ate the same circumscribed diet every day and traded in contraband snacks.

Gene stared out the small, dark windows as first Rotherford, then Janz, gave speeches — about the vision of this fortress, its strategic mission for the vehicles traversing these dangerous depths, a refuge of plenty and light, the many scientific discoveries by its dedicated staff, and now Dr. Eugenie Borometz, following in her famous mother's footsteps, would —

Gene absently covered her ears; the thrum had gone past irritation and into pain. And just as she registered the soldiers around her doing the same, the *thing* struck.

The window held, but the entire nanoceramic, steel-reinforced room rang like a bell, throwing everyone to the floor. Gene got her Vancouver-trained earthquake gait on, crouching, ankles under hips, and staggered swiftly across the room to get Rotherford, his head bleeding from the sharp edge of the podium.

He mumbled urgently into her ear as she got an arm around him, helping Janz get the old man to his feet. "Don't look, don't look at it," he whispered, tangling his fingers in her dark curls. "Don't look, Effie!"

The room filled with shouts, curses, roars of rage and pain. As they piled for the doors before they could seal shut, the thing collided again and stuck. Gene froze, words emptying from her mind.

It looked as if part of the ocean itself had torn free — long curls of black muscle, viscous with transparent slime, a blue glow pulsing from rows of bulbous ovoids, not quite tentacles, not quite limbs. Transparent fangs scrabbled at the plexiglass. The darkness of the ocean through the windows spangled suddenly with cracks, as if a bubble had popped.

"Run!" Janz shouted, pulling her arm.

Long arms squeezed through the broken plastic, dripping blue blood and glowing liquid. A private vanished screaming thorough one of the holes, his body briefly stemming the flood of seawater.

"It won't stop," she said, barely audible over the roar of the water, the cries of people wading through the knee-deep water, some panicking and already starting to swim, tangling in the tables and chairs. More limbs forced their way in, the metal between the windows creaking, preparing to admit the entire monster and its gaping, glass-fanged mouth. Its eyes were voids, starry-black, huge and apparently sightless, padded in acres of pulpy flesh. "Janz. Janz!

It won't stop!"

Drive it off, quick. Maybe not kill it, but scare it, hurt it. Negative response, aversion training. Quick. She shook Janz loose and snatched his service weapon, an electric shock-stick, off its holster. Someone tall — there. A young private waded past her; she snatched at his jacket, swinging him around. "Get up on that table," she hissed. "And give me a boost."

That was the problem with soldiers, really; they simply shut down and did what they were told. Balanced atop his sopping, bony shoulders, Gene jumped and got one hand on the red pipeline in the ceiling marked 'DANGER.' It snapped loose, hissing its stench past her face, the mercaptan marker of the fort's homegrown biogas. Couldn't be helped. She held her breath and thumbed the button on Janz' weapon.

⚘⚘⚘

She came to in the medical room with one of the doctor's assistants, a tough-looking kid whose hands shook as she went from bed to bed administering morphine and stitching cuts.

"What happened?" Gene said, her voice tinny and far-away.

"A miracle, I think," the girl said. "If the stories I'm hearing are true. Here, hold this. Your ears are still bleeding."

Gene pressed on the cotton and listened to the girl talk — the fireball, the thing's remains fading into darkness, the cascading water, their hairsbreadth escape. Eight bodies, twenty-five missing, including Dr. Wong. Disaster, death, despair. Someone would have to come evacuate them now, right? Right?

Locked tight in her quarters, Gene logged on to the sturdy, military-style computer and tried to think of what to tell her mother. Nothing seemed either right or sane. *We heard it screaming before it arrived.*

Finally, she closed her email and opened a search window, trembling fingers finding the ROT's bare spot of ocean on the map, boxing it off. Should have done it before she'd left. Might have said no. They didn't need a scientist, she thought. Not someone who knew what was down here. What they needed, they could not get from her.

Shipwrecks dating back hundreds of years; vast floating rafts

165

of dead abyssal fish; deep-sea vents vanished between monthly visits; weapons tests gone wrong, no reasons ever found; elders from the closest islands, hundreds of miles away, forbidding their people to cross this place for war or bounty; typhoons that erupted from nowhere to destroy entire fleets; GPS tracking tags on mantas and whales disappearing into the black hole of despair that centered here. Right here. *Right here.*

Gene's back prickled with sweat. It was not the deepest part of the ocean, but it was the darkest. Why had they sent her here? Why anyone?

General Rotherford was back in his office rather than quarters, as she'd guessed. He glanced up as she came in, his face all angles for a moment, skull-like, as if he were only half of himself without his usual entourage.

"That thing," she began, and stopped. Everything sounded wrong again.

Rotherford seemed to know what she meant. "Nothing I've seen before," he said. "But I think the important thing is that you killed it."

"Me and that tall, skinny guy," she said. "Is he OK?"

"Hm? Oh. Yeah. Good swimmer, that guy. Good thing, too." He toyed with the ancient, hard-lined phone on his desk. Somewhere nearby, something was dripping, a constant, irregular sound. Everything was molding and crumbling here, everything was creaking under the pressure of the billions of tons of ocean. This was no place for science. No place for humans, with their soft, undefended skin, their lack of claws and fangs, their delicate bones. "I contacted the Foundation," Rotherford said, still not meeting her gaze. "They're coming for you in about seventy-two hours, their best guess. I'll have the guys give the ROV a once-over. Check the autopilot."

"That *thing*," she said again, drawing it out. "You knew what it was."

"Of course not."

"You... you said, even before you saw it. Before any of us did. You said, 'Don't look, don't look.' Why?"

"I didn't say that," he said, the confusion in his voice apparently genuine. The dark marks under his eyes looked not like bruises but paint, as if he might never get rid of them. "How are your ears? You were awful close to that flash."

"Better. And I can color in my eyebrows with a Sharpie for a while."

He came around the desk, moving so that she had to back up till she was out the door. "The important thing is that it's dead," he said. "And that you can go home. Isn't that it? I can look over your report before you go."

"General Rotherford, I can't write a full report in three d — "

"No problem; we've got good internet down here, you know. Anything you need, just let me know."

After a few hazy, nightmare-filled hours of sleep, she gulped her hoarded sedatives and managed to stay under till almost mid-day. Without maps in the ROT, she relied on memory to reach the sample room, where the creature's remains had been carefully bottled — less than she had expected, but maybe her expectations were all off, because when had she killed anything with a fireball before?

The amber bottle contained nothing resembling the remains of anything she'd ever studied. Just a formless darkness, as if it were filled with ink or blood, separating into clotted layers. The blue luminescence she remembered from those crazed moments before the detonation was gone now, the bacteria dead now that their host had died. She reached for it, then drew her hand back. There was a whole setup in the corner — microscopes, scalpels, forceps, slides, a big, expensive monitor — but she didn't want to open the jar, let alone look at its contents. And the idea of touching it...

Abruptly she shoved herself back from the counter. The Telltale Blob, she thought. Beating though it was dead, beating through the floorboards, and no sound at all except in the mind. She'd seen that before, on long research voyages: isolated from the rest of the world, living under the crushing pressure and darkness, growing ever more aware of how fragile you were. More fragile than the jellies, the feathery tube-worms, which had evolved to be here and had earned their place. Unlike pitiful *humans*, who should be driven out, or if not, then subjugated to the real denizens of the deep, living in servitude to the superior things of the deep, the rulers of the...

She stopped short, fingers slack on the door handle. Where had that thought come from? Rulers indeed. As if a jarful of dead,

167

black tissue could be a ruler of anything.

The next morning, she went to Oscar's, hoping to see General Rotherford there now that both dining rooms had been destroyed. The few soldiers she'd spoken to the day before had seemed — what was the old word for it? — *Shellshocked*, yes, numb, unable to follow simple orders, wanting only to sleep and obsessively pre-plan routes to the armory: "In case it comes back."

"It won't come back," she told them. "It can't." The scientists nodded; the soldiers seemed unsure. And then both had changed the subject, ashamed of their fear.

Gene joined Rotherford and Ruiz, enjoying the general mess' subdued, utilitarian atmosphere — fluorescent lights, benched tables. Rotherford looked at her with a curious shyness, eyes strangely clouded, as she sat next to him with her oatmeal.

"How's your report coming?" he said.

"General, there's something you're not telling me," she said. "I don't know what. But something you should have told me before I came. Not after."

Ruiz was staring at her, scrambled egg jiggling on the end of her fork like the Jell-O in that old movie.

"General," Gene said again, into the silence.

"I will not confess," he said.

"You didn't say 'There is nothing to confess,'" Gene said.

"No," he said. "I didn't."

Something strange and cold stole over her. He always said what he meant to say, her mother had said, on one of her rare trips down memory lane. Not what he thought others wanted to hear. Always.

Two more days and she would be gone. Was it worth it to speak up now, with the threat gone before she could even analyze it? With nothing left but that single jar, and the expectation of a report? And yet, the look in his eyes: not merely fear but cloud, as if in a single day he had developed cataracts, greenish-grey over his blue irises.

"You checked out those ruins yourself," she said.

He pushed his bowl aside and stood. She waited for him to say: They're not ruins. They're cooled stone, they're pareidolia. You're seeing buildings where none could have been built. You did not see what you claimed to see.

And then she could have said, "Nor did you," but the conversation they were not having was interrupted, as she had known it would be, by a blaring alarm.

Everyone scattered, cutlery ringing to the floor. She too stood, her face an inch from the general's. Something finally flashed across the dull eyes — not cunning exactly, or hope, but some uncanny mix of the two, suggesting not malicious intent but a plan. Whatever your plan, you will be too late, old man, she told him with her eyes, and then fled with the others.

Ruiz seized her just outside the door, and Gene panicked for a moment — part of the conspiracy of silence? harm meant? — the instantaneous calculus of risk from a woman in a strange and unfamiliar place, but Ruiz' face was set in the blinking red lights. "I'm arming you," she said. "This way."

"The armory is — "

"Nothing from the armory will kill what's coming," she said.

"So, you knew too," Gene said, unable to help it.

"Knew? No. Not till you got here, till you called him on it. Guessed."

"We're scientists," Gene said. "What's coming, can we explain it with science? We can't, can we?"

"Keep up, doctor," Ruiz replied grimly.

☠ ☠ ☠

"You were supposed to kill it!" someone screamed, no face, just a whirling mass of blood and navy uniform. "They brought you to kill it!"

"It's dead!" Gene shouted, her words cut off by a blow to the stomach, so unexpected that it not merely winded her but threw her halfway across the rec room, landing in a foot of seawater. What had hit her? The room was a maelstrom of dashing bodies, the bright flashes of electrical weapons — just as in space, they had a great fear of projectiles, anything that might breach their precious equilibrium and allow the ocean to crush them, the outside coming in instead of the inside being slurped out.

Voices raged, impossible to tell whether it was an exchange or random scraps of a longer debate: "It wasn't dead! They lied to us!" "Duck!" "It *was* dead! This is something else!" "Bull*shit*! Look

169

at it!" "Don't make me look at it!"

Don't look, don't look, thought Gene, and fought her way to the far wall using the butt of the weapon they'd stolen from the armory. Fear this new menace. Even the menace of the thing she now cradled — "The General knew," Ruiz had said. Somehow, he knew, and had, long ago, she'd explained, designed this weapon himself, telling no one. Never intending to use it. But there were no secrets in a fortress.

They'd had to break into the weapon's secret room with a fire axe, setting off clumsily rigged homebrew alarms. Crude or not, the General would have been alerted — but, where was he? We left him behind, Gene thought. And now he's out there somewhere. An object of fear or guilt, that we abandoned an old man, that now we've lost track of an enemy.

Ruiz fell at her side, yanking at Gene's jacket; they dropped into the icy saltwater already leaking into the room from the cracked walls, bowing under the repeated blows of the still-unseen monster. A second later Gene heard the whizz-crack of the tasers over her head, embedding themselves with shocking depth into the air hockey table.

She rolled, kicking weakly at the shooter, just as Ruiz launched herself from the water like a breaching shark. They tangled, fetched up spluttering against the wall as Gene splashed after them.

She ripped off the man's askew hat, revealing not the General but Janz, eyes bright with both panic and a hot fanaticism quite at odds from the General's bland acceptance. "He sent you to off us!" Ruiz yelled, scruffing the man with unexpected ferocity. Gene slapped the taser out of his limp hands, and Ruiz turned him loose.

"Not kill you!" Janz gasped. "He didn't say kill. He said...he said just...stop you from doing what you were going to do."

"How did he know what we were going to do?" Gene said. "For all he knew, we were going to evacuate to the other end of the station with everybody else."

"No," Janz said. "He said you knew too much. Whatever it was you knew. It was too much. I don't know, I don't *know*, doctor, I don't — "

Ruiz cracked him across the face, hard but without malice. "We're in the battlefield here," she said, an inch from his nose. "And you're a soldier. Focus. What did the general tell you?"

"He told you the truth about these things," Gene said slowly. "Didn't he. That he created them. That the weapons testing you did down here..."

"No!"

"And he couldn't tell anyone else," Gene said. "Didn't trust them. Because even *you* don't know what you're testing sometimes. Do you. Because — "

"No." A gravelly whisper from behind her, a second before the cobbled-together weapon was yanked away. The shoulder strap tangled, sending her to her knees. The water she spat out as she rose had a new taste — not just salt but something acrid and rotten.

"What were you testing?" Gene snapped. The monster outside was still hammering on the reinforced walls, every sound ringing through the struts and beams, transmitting itself into her very fingertips. "You *knew* something lived here, right here, you knew there were hundreds of years of reports, and you had the facility built *right here* — "

"We did not make them," the General said, caressing the weapon's aluminum surface, studded with black plastic rivets. "Not we, the human race...how could we? So puny as to be unnoticeable to those more worthy, how could we have created them? Nothing can make a thing more complex than itself, we all know it, they know it."

"Wh... what are you..."

The wall next to them began to cave, a tentacle forcing into the breach, tearing its eager flesh on the edges of the nanoceramic. Gene edged away.

"In my dreams they came to me," the General went on, rocking the weapon in his arms. "They are older than us, you know; once thought the reviled spawn of Cain, sent to live in the deepest dark as penance for his sin...cursed, whatever they were, cursed, sent far from God, from the glance of the holy — "

"General," Gene cut in, reaching for the weapon again, knowing he wouldn't point it at her, "give me that, please."

He jerked backwards, not alarmed yet, his face slack, homicidal, dreamy. "They are within me," he said. "Not found by me, not concealed by me, not controlled. *Within*. In dreams they came, offered me a place — powerful, ancient... you don't know how powerful, you cannot. You think they are destroying this place? No, they only seek to show their dominance, because we offended them, we committed blasphemy with our noises and our tests and our submarines and our lights, we blasphemed against them, against *Her*, against Her son — and now you have killed him — "

"What?"

"— and you seek to kill Her, and I won't let you, I cannot..."

"Then why did you make that gun, General?"

His voice sank as he mumbled, still caressing the thing. And Gene finally understood: He was so convinced that these creatures were speaking to him, or had some kind of power over him, that he could never destroy them himself, and someone else would have to pull the trigger when the day came that his delusion was challenged. Some tiny spark of sanity, Gene thought, still lived down there, in his own darkness, in his own ruins.

"They will return one day, all of them, from their hidden places," Rotherford said, still backing away, heading for the door. "And when they do, I will be...I will be upheld most greatly, I will be not merely prince or lord but king, emperor, dictator, and my human body — "

"General - "

"They are Gods, Effie," he whispered, fumbling for the door pad. She finally broke from her frozen fascination and waded towards him, Ruiz and Janz in pursuit. "More ancient than any of man's gods, more ancient than the universe's old gods, and they have blessed our planet with their presence, and... and... they have given me knowledge, great and secret knowledge..."

"General Rotherford," she said, holding her hands out, "it's me. It's Eugenie. Not Ephigenia. She's not here, she didn't come. It's just me. I'm all you've got."

"No, they are... She promised me..."

"General — *Theo* — you're sick, you're not well. No, not sick. You're fine. You're... you hit your head yesterday, remember? Give me the weapon, we'll help you get better — "

He'd have to turn to fit through the doorway. And when he did —

— but something snapped around her ankle, and she crashed into the water again, a sour blackness closing over her head. In the turmoil it took a near-fatal moment to realize that she was moving, yanked through the water, banging against tables, chairs, boots, water being forced up her nose; she couldn't raise her head to breathe. Drowned by dragging, she thought. Like being keelhauled. A bubbling blackness, dark sparkles growing.

At last her hand clenched on a table leg, nearly yanking her arm out of the socket. The hold on her ankle slipped free, and she jerked her head above surface, coughing out a stream of seawater.

Through red-tinted eyes she saw everything in a brief, dark tableau: the tentacle searching again for her leg, pulsating and glowing; the eyes on the far side of the ripped wall, holding back the water, dozens upon dozens of eyes, perhaps hundreds, huge, vermilion and gold, as if a sunset had sunk to the abyssal plain.

Something roared, so abrupt and loud she screamed reflexively, hands coming up to cover her ears. The tentacle snaked up from the water, swayed like a snake; dozens of similar snakes rose from the surface, interested, listening, as if they were charmed. Were they watching her? Gene couldn't tear herself away from their gaze, stunned by the noise, the jumbled syllables in her head slowly resolving themselves into words — not, she realized, through anything happening in her head. The thing (*Her?*) continued to force its way in, mere feet from her.

This close, she could study it as if it were a blurry photo from a rover installing cables miles below the surface or something a friend had found on the internet. Not a fish, not a cephalopod, despite the tentacles; not a whale, not a shark, not a ray. Not anything. Not, perhaps, an animal at all, not if it could talk.

No, it couldn't be talking. I see now, she almost cried out. The pressure, the darkness, the isolation, your brain made it speak — and it did truly speak, in what it probably thought was a conspiratorial whisper but was truly a scream: *"We could spare you, if you but swear yourself to us, as did the other, the first, our first convert, our first apostle, you could be another, spread our word, our glad tidings, we return to rise up, even for the death of my spawn you could be forgiven, if you but take down the gates in your mind and let us in, let us ride you, as in days of old — "*

Gene backed away from the wall, the staring eyes. Someone had rallied their nerves and a few soldiers to slap at the wet tentacles with their service weapons, screaming silently at mishits or friendly fire, filling the air with a chemical stench.

Not betrayed so much as defrauded, she thought. He didn't lure me down here with the promise of apostleship, but he didn't put it outside the realm of possibility, either. He just didn't think that I might actually kill one of his gods...

For Chrissake, Gene! It's not really a god! Don't call it that! You're a scientist! What kind of god would act like that?

Well. An old one, for starters. A dangerous one. One whose existence is, right here, right now, incompatible with those it wishes to convert. That kind of god.

I have to do something.

I did not come here saying I could do this thing. But he knew I could, all the same.

A sudden silence fell, the thing outside ceasing its communication. Kraken, Charybdis, Leviathan, she thought, swimming away from the cracking, creaking walls, the baleful stare. Nothing man could kill. Gods indeed, or half-gods, only to be killed by something with a touch of the divine. But if the general's weapon really worked — untested, hidden, like a nuclear deterrent —

"Gene!" someone screamed behind her, and without even looking she put her arms over her head and sank into the icy water. Electricity crackled overhead. Ruiz had warned her; she must have tried to stop the General from leaving, finish what Gene couldn't.

Unseeing, Gene fumbled for the banana knife in her boot. It had once been her mother's, usually used for slicing sediment samples off augers or prying barnacles off hulls, the blade keen and old and deadly. She surged up from the water and calmly surfaced between Ruiz and the general, who immediately lowered his weapon, unable to keep both the shock baton and the god-killing kludged gun upright at once. She didn't know if she could kill him, but she'd used the knife enough to know that she could damn sure hurt him. His face didn't seem to register that as she raised her arm.

"In Her name," he said calmly, and something slammed between them, a slimy black wall glowing and crawling with blue glyphs, suckers and claws pulsating, as unyielding as marble. How had it known to protect him?

It didn't matter. She dug the knife in and dragged it down, putting her full weight into it, barely scoring the rubbery skin.

"She cannot be harmed by human means," Janz said behind her; she turned, seeing his wild, glassy eyes. Another convert, she thought. No. Another victim of this undersea hysteria. She hoisted the knife again just as the lights went out, leaving them in darkness lit only by the blue bioluminescence of the tentacle.

Which slowly, crawlingly, began to resolve themselves into patterns...letters...then words. Gene froze, Janz at her side, his hand moving caressingly over the hard, slimy skin. *Join us*, it wrote. *See our power. Doubt no more.*

And in a flash she saw what it must have shown the General before it stole his mind — the Earth's oceans boiling with creatures, heaving onto land, destroying cities, mushroom clouds sprouting, but always the dark water birthing more, trailing limbs and fangs and spines, the ancient temples rising, sediment sheeting off them like water, monstrous eyes opening, awakening from sleeps so long that human memory had erased it, swimming from their ruins, the source of their —

—the ruins.

Gene snapped her head around, then clenched her hand around the knife. A grappling hook? She dug the tip into the slippery skin and used it to haul herself over the tentacle, scrabbling desperately at the top. It was so dim — where was the General?

She triangulated based on Ruiz' cries, and launched herself from the summit, wrenching the great weapon free as she held his head underwater. The tentacle instantly retracted out of her target range, just as she'd hoped. She spun, trying to get her bearings, then aimed at a blank spot on the wall.

The weapon had no kick whatsoever (what in the *hell* had the old man designed?) but emitted a basketball-sized sphere of blue plasma that sliced a perfect disc out of the wall, scooping a small wedge of flesh from the writhing tentacle and continuing across the black water barely dimmed...until it detonated against the base of the ruins, the blue spreading in circles, a shockwave that made the entire fortress tremble.

Janz and the General had vanished in the chaos; she fought her way past the rapidly retreating tentacles to find Ruiz, impossibly, still wedging the door open. They kicked the block loose as they fled, doors slamming shut behind them.

The pod's autopilot had been damaged, but she could still follow the flotilla of lifeboats making their slow way towards the surface; behind her, identically stinking of blood, seawater, and the black-brimming jar she'd insisted they bring, Ruiz exhaustedly kept on the headlight, watching for anything large in the water.

"Did that really just happen?" she would say occasionally, and Gene would reply, "Keep it together, Ruiz." Whenever she glanced back, Ruiz was cradling the jar close, even resting her chin on the lid, as if listening to it.

"What will we tell the Foundation?"

"I don't know," Gene said.

"That thing," Ruiz said. "Do you think it was really a... a god? Like the General said?"

"Yes."

"But we're scientists. We can't..."

"I know," Gene said grimly, focusing on keeping the lifepods in sight.

"So, what happens now? We killed a god, we destroyed its...its church, its temple..."

"We run and keep running," Gene said. "And we hope we can run far and fast enough."

They fell silent, limping through the black water. Far below, the light touched the edge of the blast crater where the ruins had lain, still shimmering with the blood of destroyed monsters.

THE DEEP

by Donna Leahey

Landwalkers killed the queen of the sea. Dragged her body into the sky with a chain, her blood raining down upon us. We cried at them to release her, but, as always, they ignored us. The tiny killers, the Landwalkers, those who invade our realm celebrate while her life twitches away. They drag her from her home with a motor spilling foul-tasting oil into the sea. Her majestic bulk, once graceful and glorious, hung lifeless in the hooks and ropes as they swarmed over her, cutting into her still quivering flesh.

The blue whales sing their sorrow into the sea. *The queen! Lament! She sings no more!*

Her pod adds the first angry notes. *Murdered!* Their powerful voices, booming and deep, cut through the mourning, warbling through the constant hum and rumble of the sea.

She is gone, she is gone! The notes carry through the water, thrumming through the deep waves, spreading the word. Even those of us not of her kind mourn her. None of us are old enough to remember a time she hadn't swum the currents.

Her kind pound the beats of anger. *Murdered! Killed!*

My pod and I dove deeper and deeper, hoping our squeals of mercy for the Landwalkers would be heard, but not even all agreed. *They take us from our family. They trap us away from the sea.*

The orca agree. *They take us. They imprison us. We die. Our calves die, never knowing the sea.*

We don't know where the first cries of *the Deep* rang out, but soon the sea was alive with the whale's call for vengeance. The few dissenting voices, like my own, swept aside in the rising tide of rage.

Summon the Deep!

I have always played in the waves their ships forge in the sea. I have leapt into the sky to hear their cries, twisting and cavorting for them. Landwalkers saved me when I was a pup. I'd foolishly swum too close to the beach. I lay there, trapped on the sand as the tide rolled out. Even my mother lost hope as the waves drove her farther and farther from me. Then they came, splashed water on my parched skin and pulled me out into the water until I could swim away and rejoin my mother.

I've heard of other pups stolen from the water and held on land until they died. I wail for them, but that is not what I know of the Landwalkers. I still swim because of them.

I return to the surface for a lungful of air and dive again. Songs that have never been sung before ripple through the depths seeking the most ancient protectors of the sea.

I cry out. *Wait! Give warning! Their pups are innocent. There are so many who do not deserve this fate.* I hope others will take up my cry, repeat it.

But only the blues answer. *They killed the queen. Vengeance.*

The Landwalkers hear the songs of the Deep and fury but don't understand, and so they do exactly what they should not have: they come out into the waters. Their ships and their noisy submarines gather round the singing whales.

Don't they hear the rumbling sound of their deaths awakening?

The sea becomes cloudy with silt stirring from the depths. Silt and debris that hasn't seen light in millennia. Shadows, dark and amorphous, move underneath. And more Landwalkers come.

Go! Flee! I cry warning to the creatures on a giant ship. I leap into the sky and dance and sing for their attention. They point, they laugh, they squeal unintelligibly. But they do not go. There are so many of them. They should go to land, where they may be safe.

But they do not listen.

The giants sing, diving as deep as their bodies can stand and emerging only to breathe before they return to their songs. In every sea, the song has spread, repeated over and over, calling down into the darkness, rousing the dark ones. *The Deep. The Deep.*

An underwater ship full of Landwalkers rumbles closer to the singers. I swim closer, unsure how to warn them away. The sea is full of ancient and musty silt, and I can feel the Deep growing ever closer. They must go before it's too late.

The ship is too deep for me, but I dive towards it anyway, clicking and squealing my warning. The shadows uncoil beneath it.

That shell full of air and Landwalkers is more fragile than they know. The water presses on me; I am too deep. I turn back towards the sky.

A sharp crack and a boom reverberate through the water, and I cannot see. Bubbles of air cascade around me, then clear to reveal the fragile ship crushed in the very tip of a tentacle. A Landwalker, frantic for life, thrashes fruitlessly while others float motionless near it, their bodies mangled and bloody. The tentacle flexes, and the shell breaks apart completely, releasing more air and strange, foul-tasting fluids. The tentacle drops the halves of the submarine and it vanishes into the depths. The Landwalker ends its fight for life and air far from the sky it lives in. The tentacle vanishes into the gloom.

The whales' songs boom through the currents. *The Deep is here. The waters will be ours again.*

A Landwalker, lifeless and quiet, floats upward. One limb is mangled, another missing entirely. Its red blood streams into the currents around us, but I doubt any sharks will come. They have likely fled the Deep. The Landwalker's eyes stare sightlessly towards the sky, its strange mouth gapes open. Did it have pups who will wonder why it never came home? A wave of sorrow washes through me and I turn skyward.

The urge to breathe grows stronger, a pressure in my body. My tail pushes against the water until I leap into the air, arcing high to see above the surface. More of the Landwalker ships have come. Instead of being warned away by the whale song, they have been drawn to it. In the distance, I see their behemoth of a ship—the kind their planes launch from. The Landwalkers watch us watching them. They don't understand.

You must go back to your land! I cry, but the Landwalkers have never understood us. They point at us, at the others who have risen to the surface, but they don't heed our warnings.

Why? Why? A whale sings at me. *Let them drown.*

The water churns around us from the force of the rising destruction. Their planes begin to launch, but it is too late for them. For all of them. A tentacle, dark and dripping the ancient silt that it carried up from the darkness with it, rises up and slams down. The enormous ship lists towards the tentacle and another grabs at it, and another. The first tentacle wraps entirely around the ship, pulling it into the waves. Several of the planes fall, sinking into the depths. A tentacle grabs one and flings it into the sky, but it doesn't take wing and fly, it just falls again into the roiling waves, cutting downward through the water as it once cut upward through the sky. A Landwalker caught inside stares, motionless, at the tentacles as it sinks into the murky darkness.

It is followed by a chunk of the giant ship as large as one of the watching whales. The wreckage tumbles out of sight in a cascade of bubbles and debris and bloody pieces of Landwalkers. The ones not yet dead wail in shrieks and moans much like the songs of the whales deep below.

One of my kind, a stranger from another pod, flees, her eyes terrified, her tail flailing. Behind her blowhole is a horrible scar, a misshapen chunk of flesh ripped from her and healed badly, an artifact no doubt of swimming too close to a propeller-driven ship.

Help me! I click to her, I squeal. *Help me warn the Landwalkers?*

The stranger veers slightly at my call, then lashes her tail even more furiously as her hurried clicks travel back to me. *Let the sea take them. They earned this fate.*

Not all! I call after her, but it is too late. The water is too dark, too full of ancient silt. She is gone.

The water churns about me, growing ever colder as the Deep rises below me. I flee towards land. It is too late for the ships on the open sea, but perhaps the ones nearer their home can be warned.

I seek the currents, the tastes that will lead me to land, but the sea is too angry. The rise of the Deep has muddied the waters far too much. I rise to the surface, breathe deeply, and dive again, hoping I am headed towards the shore. The image of the enormous ship cracked and broken, its pieces vanishing beneath the waves, sears onto my mind. Worse, the anguished cries of the Landwalkers as they face their deaths in the cold of the sea ring endlessly through my mind.

I race on, my body cutting through the water, my tail pushing against the turbulent current with all my strength. I rise to the surface, breathe, dive, and swim on in a cycle that repeats until I emerge and see lights. I have found the shore. Now to warn the Landwalkers.

I leap from the waves, which grow more frenzied by the moment. I squeal and click, trying to urge the small ships to shore.

They ignore me. I rush toward the nearest ship as three Landwalkers lean over the edge, watching me. They wave their limbs at me and cry out, but do not heed my warning.

I dive, in preparation to leap even higher, but am jerked to a stop when something grabs my fin.

I attempt to dart away but cannot escape. At first, I cannot see what has me, a shark, or perhaps one of the arms of the Deep, but it is some *thing* of the Landwalkers. I struggle to escape, but only succeed in becoming more entangled in whatever this is. Its strands bite into my flesh and confine my limbs. My own blood trickles upward as it bites into me. The pain is not as bad as the fear. I am caught and the Deep of the sea is coming.

I continue to fight to be free as it drags me against my will, and I understand at last that whatever has me is part of the ship I had hoped to warn. Fish, shellfish, even a small shark are trapped in its grasp with me. The more I fight, the tighter it holds me until I am entirely wrapped in its embrace. I cannot move. I cannot swim.

I cry out for help, wailing into the sea.

No help comes.

I need to take a breath, but no amount of thrashing brings me closer to the air. My body craves it, the one thing I cannot find beneath the waves. Air.

My vision grows dark as my lungs ache, my body cries out. No, it is not my vision, it is the water. The water grows cloudy with murk. The Deep is coming.

I become frantic. I would give anything for one tiny sip of air. One bubble.

A tentacle appears from the murk. It is not here to save me. It is here to kill the Landwalkers.

I cannot stop myself. Water flows into my lungs. My body convulses. The tentacle reaches past me to crush the ship.

They have done this to themselves.

The world goes black.

OUT GHENT LAKE

by Darren Todd

It's no wonder to me how some things stay hidden in this world. People don't believe in ghosts or Bigfoot because they think—if they really existed—someone would have exposed them by now. That modern times would shine a light on anything like that and every person on the planet would know about it in hours, thanks to the internet.

They even got a name for them: cryptids. It means creatures whose existence is unproven. But if you look at where the word came from—the Greek—it just means hidden. A hidden creature.

I realize whatever lives in Ghent Lake will never take over the world. It's not even going to take over tiny little Rextown ten miles away. That's because whatever's under that black water is patient. It doesn't care if people believe in it. But those few who do—mostly the old-timers—they think there's only one of them, but I know different. Cause Daddy killed one, and… well, what happened after meant there was more than one to begin with.

I was reading, just a little girl. About halfway through Judy Blume's book *Are You There God? It's Me, Margaret* which was way bigger than *Otherwise Known as Sheila the Great* and kinda sad and serious, but I still liked it. Daddy was driving us back from the beach. We'd spent the whole weekend on the coast: me, my little brother Jimmy, and my parents. Momma was sleeping, her elbow out the window. We were going fast enough for the wind coming past Momma to flutter the pages of my book, so I had to hold them down.

Jimmy had bought one of those toy sharks that you wind up so it swims underwater. Daddy had told him he'd lose it in about a second in the ocean, but somehow he kept finding it. Now, even with no more water to swim in, he'd wind that thing up and dangle it by the dorsal fin, guiding it around the back seat, patrolling for prey.

The gears made this clicking noise as they turned, kinda annoying, but Daddy put jazz on the radio, and that drowned most of it out.

We were only about twenty minutes from home when Daddy stomped the brakes, sending me and Jimmy flying down behind the front seats. Momma gasped awake but must have braced herself just in time to keep from banging her head on the dash. A second later, the car hit something. We'd run into a deer once before, while we were driving to see my grandpa in Virginia. It had sounded like we'd hit a giant sack of flour. But this sounded different: a mixture of squishing and bumping, as if we'd smashed into a giant Jell-O mold.

I didn't worry about what it was at that moment. I just wanted to get myself up from the floorboards and make sure no one was hurt. Our old Buick guzzled gas, but it rode as smooth as a puck over ice. Thing was, none of us were wearing seatbelts. Hardly anybody did back then.

"Everyone all right?" Daddy asked. He put his arm behind Momma like he did when backing out of a parking space, only now I saw panic in his eyes. That scared me more than the accident. I nodded my head, and he turned to Jimmy. "How 'bout you, champ. Y'okay?"

"I fell on my shark," Jimmy whined. "Now his fin's all crooked."

"Jimmy, I don't care about some silly shark," Momma told him. "Are you hurt?"

"No, ma'am," he said.

"What happened?" Momma asked. I know she must have been tired from chasing us around and being in the sun all day, but I remember she looked beautiful. She'd pulled her hair into a high pony tail, which she never did. And her pinkish shoulders barely held up the cotton blouse she wore over her bikini top. She had on these big sunglasses with the gradient tint—blue-black up top and then a violet, almost clear on the bottom. "Did we get a flat tire?"

"We hit something," Daddy said, turning back around.

"Oh, no," Momma said. "What was it?"

Daddy hunched over the steering wheel, like he was studying the gauges, but I could tell that wasn't it. Then he looked past us, over his shoulder. "Not sure. Some kind of animal."

Jimmy and I whipped around, trying to catch sight of

whatever we'd hit. We'd been driving west, back home from the coast, with the sun highlighting the road behind us clear as a picture. And yet it lay empty, no animal and not even a smear of blood. The only evidence was the set of black marks from where Daddy had locked up the tires.

Momma said, "You think it was—"

Then a horrible crunching noise came from the front of the car, like the Buick had forgotten to react to the collision and only now did so. We could run over a pothole and feel nothing in that tank, and yet with every crunch it shook on the frame, as if an eighteen-wheeler were flying by every few seconds.

"Daddy," I said, and he must have heard something in my tone, 'cause he turned and held out a hand to both of us.

"It's fine," he said. He looked to Momma. "Sit tight."

That stretch of Old Hannah Road ended at Rextown, tapering off to little more than a gravel drive heading west out of town past that. So we were unlikely to see much traffic, not unless it was another family coming back from the beach, and most of them would only spend Saturdays on the coast. On account of us not going to church (Daddy was never a God-fearing man), we'd stay through Sunday and have most of the beach to ourselves.

To the south a copse of trees huddled together like they were co-conspirators, and I guess they were. Ghent Lake sat behind them, only you'd never tell from the road, both 'cause of that tree line and 'cause no signs told you so. Everybody from Rextown knew it was there, but most figured they were better off not thinking about it.

Only, when Daddy got out and rounded the corner of the car to see what was making that terrible noise, the lake was *all* I could think about. No one from Rextown visited the lake because they all knew better. You could swim there a thousand times and nothing would happen, but one too many kids had disappeared over the years to call it coincidence. They'd dragged the bottom, of course. Twice, I think. Even hired a couple of divers from off the coast. They might have figured the kids wandered off. Only the missing always left stuff behind. Clothes, radios, sunglasses. Stuff that the teenagers— the only dummies swimming at Ghent at all—wouldn't want to get wet. I guess they found their cars, too. Like I said, it never happened enough to put all the pieces together.

But something about that copse of trees bothered me. I

scanned the tree line and my brain finally caught up with my eyes. A handful of saplings were bent double, snapped at about waist level. The weeds on the strip of ground between the road and the trees were all smushed, like something had just walked through them. Only it didn't look like any path a deer would make, or a person for that matter. It looked wider than that, sloppy too, like if you'd rolled a boulder end over end. The trail stopped at the asphalt, and I followed it to where Daddy had made those rubber tracks from braking so hard.

"Daddy," I yelled and spun to find him standing at the front of the car. Maybe Momma couldn't see it, sitting high up in her seat and with the visor down, but from low in the back, I could see his face. It wore a mix of horror and disgust, but all that topped with raw fear. I don't know what he was looking at, but that crunching noise came again, and a single, thick tentacle slapped the hood of the car with such force it sounded like thunder.

That was when I screamed, and it only took about a second before Jimmy joined in, even though he had no idea what was going on. Momma didn't make a sound, but she moved snake-fast from the front seat to the back, so quick it seemed like a movie trick. She pulled me and Jimmy toward her and coiled her arms around us. I don't remember if I kept screaming or not, but I know I kept my eyes on Daddy; I had to. They wouldn't move off him. He backed away from whatever that tentacle belonged to. He ran around, and I thought he would pull us out of the car or even get in beside us, but then he went to the trunk and opened it. The lift support grumbled when he jerked it up.

"Harold, what are you—" Momma yelled, but then another slamming noise came from the hood. I turned and saw a second tentacle folding and writhing onto the surface. The first one had crept up, straightened, and hooked itself to the top of the hood, near the windshield.

"It's coming for us," Jimmy wailed, and just like seeing Daddy scared, something about hearing that from my little brother made everything twice as terrible. I formed all these images in my head of it squirming in through the air vents and wrapping around the three of us like Momma had done. This made my chest all tight, and I couldn't seem to catch my breath. It didn't help that Momma was squeezing me so hard already.

The trunk slammed and we all jumped. Daddy stood out there—just as scared, just as panicked—only now he had that long, gross knife from the tackle box. It had a wooden handle and he'd sharpened the blade so many times it looked like a filet knife, though the metal had once been a couple inches wide. He used it to cut bait and lines and never let us kids touch it, always saying it was so sharp it would lay open our fingers just holding the thing. Daddy kept it at his side, held high, with his elbow cocked and his fist shaking, ready to stab it into anything that came near him.

Despite Momma's screaming, he walked on past the back door and around to the front. Momma yelled at him to stop, to get away. For me, the sounds had turned all muffled, like this was happening underwater. Maybe it was the same for Daddy, so he couldn't hear her calling.

He moved around, giving whatever we'd hit a wide berth at first. He stared at it for what felt like a solid minute. There was a part of me that thought he'd run. I guess every kid deep down thinks their daddy's gonna leave them one day. I never considered it before that moment, but right then, I could actually see him turning on his heels and running for town, leaving his brood to the dark fate that tentacled monster had in mind for us. If it even had a mind.

But then he was on it, my daddy. His arm shot out and stabbed at the thing all tangled up in our grill, and then the whole cab rocked and there came this awful squeal, like a pig but nothing like it, too. Same wailing, but a different tone, the difference between the trumpet player in the high school band and an air raid siren calling out incoming missiles. And it came out garbled, trilling during the wail, as if making the sound from beneath the water even while on land. Daddy pulled back and stabbed again. The thing shot out a tentacle and wrapped the slimy flesh all over his bare arm, coiling around it. It must've had little spines along it, 'cause Daddy cried out, and the three of us in the car cried along with him. Daddy stabbed again and again, the whole time yelling. His face contorted in pain one second and then fixed in utter rage the next.

I'd never seen either face on my daddy, not ever. So him going back and forth like that burned into my memory: two sides of a coin I never even knew existed but now can't ever forget.

"Stop it," Momma yelled. She couldn't take any more of it. Even if this thing meant to kill all of us, whatever changes Daddy was going through must have seemed even more terrible.

Finally, Daddy pulled back, his chest heaving, his mouth open and sucking in these deep breaths, and then the knife fell from his fingers. The tentacle that had wrapped around his arm slid off, leaving behind a beet red color to his skin, like he'd spent all day in the sun without taking cover.

The car settled on its carriage, and I heard the thing outside slide off and then plop to the ground. When Daddy opened the door and slid into the driver's seat, Momma pulled us in even tighter. Maybe she was afraid of whatever had come over Daddy, like there was no way he had anything on his mind but finishing what that monster had started.

Only, Daddy was Daddy again. From that moment on, I never worried about him leaving us again. This oily, black blood covered his shirt, and the angry red on his arms had beaded up now with his own, brighter blood. It smeared on the gray fabric of the seats. "Everyone okay?" he asked. He started the car, backed up a few feet, and took off for town before anyone answered.

Momma stared out the window as we moved off the shoulder, her mouth twitching like she was getting shocked by a live wire.

I turned to look behind us to see what Daddy had left of that creature, but Momma barked at me. "No," she said. "You don't need to see that."

"Why not, Momma?"

She looked up into the front seat at Daddy, at his eyes in the rearview mirror. I still don't know what unspoken words passed between them. All I know is that someone finding a creature on the side of the road near the lake never became a part of the legend, whether 'cause that thing was able to carry itself back to the lake before it died or something came out of that black water on after it.

"It's dead, isn't it?" I asked.

"It doesn't matter. You're safe and it's gone, so just turn yourself around and push it out of your mind."

There was no chance of that. Even when Momma let Jimmy and I sleep in bed with them, I never got a wink that night. Jimmy fell asleep long after it was full dark, but he whimpered his way through bad dream after bad dream. Momma had taken pills, I'd seen her, and maybe that was all that let her rest.

I thought Daddy was sleeping, too. He never made any noise,

not like other dads, who all snored if my friends were being truthful. In the darkness, I couldn't tell if his eyes were open. They looked like two black pools in his face.

"Darlin'?" he whispered, and I twitched like something had bitten me.

"Yes, Daddy?"

"Can't sleep either, huh?"

"No, Daddy."

"Come here," he said.

Jimmy was lying between us, but Daddy moved over to the edge of the bed, and I got out from under the covers and hopped over my brother and curled into Daddy's arm. It was the one the monster had wrapped around, that Momma had bandaged all up when we got home. Still, he winced when my head touched his bicep.

"Sorry."

"No, it's fine. Itches more than it hurts."

"Is it over, Daddy?"

He turned to look at me in the dark. His eyes still lacked any distinction, but I could tell they were open and studying me. "I'm sure of it."

Not even two weeks later, the Barston Home for Boys took a field trip out to Ghent Lake. Later, the administrator said something about how the coast was too far, and too many places in town didn't care for all those wayward boys coming all at once, even if it meant business. So he took them to the lake to reward them for good behavior. Something like they hadn't had a runaway or a fight in months. Any kid who had a Barston Home boy in their class knew how rare that was.

So they went to the lake—the papers said—and the only thing left of those boys was a dozen towels on the shore and the bus they rode in on.

I never told a soul about Daddy killing that one, probably the baby of whatever took the boys away. Not even when the manhunt started and not when it ended months later. My family kept quiet, like a lotta folks when it came to that lake.

But whenever anyone spoke of it, as if under a spell, Momma would grab me and my brother and wrap us up like we'd never left the back of that Buick. Like those tentacles were still reaching, patient and hidden.

ABOUT THE STORYTELLERS

Everyone knows that a gathering of crows is called a *murder*, but they're also called a *storytelling*. As writers, we aim to tell our stories, murdering those errors and fears that hold us back.

Please help us by reviewing this book. Whether you liked it or not, authors need your feedback and validation. It's like air.

✠✠✠

To learn more about any of the authors or projects, visit http://www.amurderofstorytellers.com.

CPSIA information can be obtained
at www.ICGtesting.com
Printed in the USA
LVHW08s2316060718
583018LV00001B/27/P

9 780692 433324